ROGUE PRINCE

KYLIE GILMORE

First Edition: October 2019

Cover design by Michele Catalano Creative

Published by: Extra Fancy Books

ISBN-10: 1-947379-21-6

ISBN-13: 978-1-947379-21-3

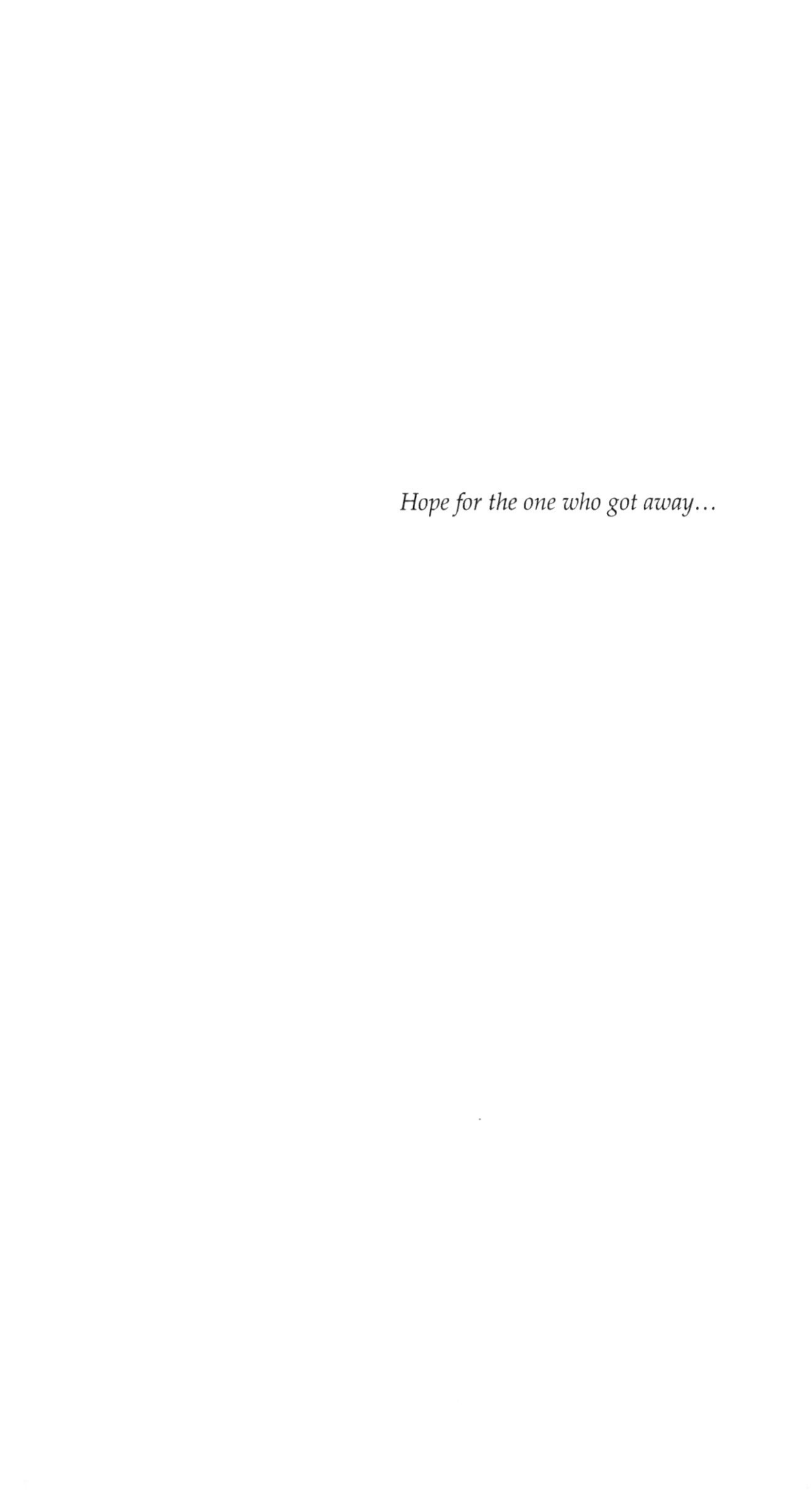

Hope for the one who got away…

$$1$$

<hr>

A few days after Christmas...Villroy Island

Dylan

How the hell did I get here? I'm standing in a rented tux in a frigging palace ballroom on Villroy Island for Prince Adrian's wedding. Me, Dylan Rourke—a construction worker from Brooklyn, New York—in a royal ballroom.

This entire palace is a monument to wealth and status. And the people in it look just as gilded, wearing designer everything. The jewels from tiaras, necklaces, bracelets, and rings glint in the light of the chandeliers.

"Shoulda brought our bling for this crowd," Sean mutters under his breath. He's my younger brother by two years, and we're tight.

I bite back a smile and say under my breath, "Gold dollar-sign necklaces will make us fit right in."

We snicker, get a few pointed looks, and get serious again. I'm pretty sure our grandparents just rolled over in their graves. See, technically, we're princes, and Adrian is our cousin. I only recently met Adrian on account of his family exiling my family due to circumstances that happened before either of us was born. This is a peacemaking mission of sorts, and it's going about as well as you'd expect.

My five younger brothers and I have managed to shock an entire ballroom of people into stunned silence. We're the elephant in the room—former exiles born from a scandalous union.

We're standing on one side of the room while everyone else in my estranged family is on the other side, staring at us. We're all waiting for the bride and groom to arrive from where they've been getting their picture taken. The stunned silence is probably because my brothers and I didn't RSVP to the wedding, though we were invited. No wedding crashing here. It was a last-minute decision to go, so we got here just in time for the reception. There was a brief scuffle trying to get into the palace, but I demanded they bring my cousin Silvia to the front hall to vouch for us.

I got to know Silvia when she moved to the US for college. Your heart would have to be made of stone not to like her. She's been on a campaign to get us to this wedding, insisting it's up to us, the younger generation, to do the hard work of bringing the family back together again. Lotta bad blood between our families. My dad had to start with nothing in Brooklyn after being raised to be king and then exiled. It was hard for him, really hard. He's still bitter about it.

Sean is the one who finally convinced me we should show up here. His reasoning was sound. If we're invited to a wedding on Villroy, then the exile is lifted. And if the exile is lifted, then maybe our business interests could align with our wealthy royal cousins' business interests. All of their business ventures have been hugely successful, from cosmetics manufacturing to a day spa to a casino. I'm not here for a handout, but if—and that's a big if—there's a reconciliation, maybe King Gabriel would give us a loan so we can start flipping houses on the weekends. Real estate development is where it's at in Brooklyn, and Sean and I want to move beyond construction. We'd pay him back with interest. It would be like a diversification for my royal cousins to have their fingers in the pie both in Villroy and Brooklyn. My dad pushed hard on the loan angle, saying it was past time our family got some of the compensation we were denied.

Now that we're here, I'm having serious doubts. Some of the older guests are looking down their noses at us. They probably knew my dad, who refused to step foot on Villroy under the circumstances. Some people are whispering in scandalous tones. Everyone is staring at us like an exhibit at the zoo.

I pull at the collar of my white dress shirt, a bead of sweat running down my spine. My brothers shift uneasily next to me. No one has approached us about our right to be here, but there's security posted around the room. Tough-looking guys with earpieces dressed all in black. Their blazers are probably concealing weapons. Will they kick us out if some of the older generation puts their foot down? I'm thinking not everyone signed off on us being here. Maybe we'll be thrown in the dungeon. Dad mentioned they have one.

I glance over at my brothers, who look grim. Going down the line from oldest to youngest, it's me, Sean, Jack, Connor, Brendan, and Garrett. Most of us have dark brown hair and blue eyes, except the youngest, Garrett, who has aquamarine eyes like our dad. Supposedly, the aquamarine eyes are a sign of a true ruler of Villroy, only that didn't work out so well for my dad.

The bride and groom finally step inside the ballroom, breaking the tension, and a cheer goes up, everyone clapping and shouting congratulations to them.

Adrian, who could pass as one of my brothers with his thick dark brown hair, sharp cheekbones, and square jaw, lifts a hand. "Thank you all for celebrating with us!" His gaze lands on me. "And a special thank-you to my cousins, who flew here all the way from New York."

I jerk my chin at him. And then Adrian surprises me, heading straight for us with his bride, Sara.

"Dylan, so good to see you here," he says, offering his hand. We met briefly in Brooklyn a few months back. He's Silvia's twin, which is why I agreed to meet him in the first place.

I shake Adrian's hand, keenly aware the room has gone silent again. "Sure. Thanks." I can't manage to say I'm glad to be here because it's awkward as hell to be the peacemaker from a cast-out family.

He introduces me to Sara, and I turn and introduce my brothers.

Silvia appears at my side. "I'm so happy you're here!" She throws her arms around me and gives me a squeeze, which is the second time she hugged me today. The first was in the front hall, where she had to get us past security. It's impossible not to like this girl when she adores me so much.

I hug her back. "I knew you'd never let me live it down if I missed it."

"And you'd be right." She beams and turns to my brothers, hugging them each in turn. Double hugs all around. It suddenly occurs to me she's hugging us here to show everyone we're accepted by the royal family. Smart. "Come on, let me introduce you to the rest of our family."

She introduces us to our great-aunt and great-uncle first, who refuse to shake my hand.

"Riffraff," the not-so-great-uncle says, pursing his lips.

My temper flares, and I clench my jaw. That's what this side of the family has called our side since the exile—riffraff. Dad told us before, but it's different hearing it right to my face. They think we're beneath them.

"I'm proud to call them family," Silvia snaps. "I'll be sure to let King Gabriel and Queen Anna know the reception you've given our honored guests."

They give us their backs. So do several other couples standing nearby. Old-school shunning. Fucking assholes. No wonder the old man is bitter.

Silvia is incensed, her cheeks flushed bright pink. "Come on. I'll introduce you to the better part of the family."

She strides across the ballroom toward the head table. My brothers and I follow at a slow pace. Coming here was a mistake. I don't know why Silvia thought we'd ever be accepted. And there's King Gabriel, sitting at the head table, looking rigid and extremely proper. That could've been me.

I'm the crown prince, firstborn son to the man who should've been king. I was born a year before Gabriel. By all rights, the throne is mine. I know it's not Gabriel's fault. This shit all went down before we were born, and I honestly can't imagine dealing with all this pompous royal stuff day in, day out. I'm a laid-back, practical guy.

"This ballroom is insane," Sean says under his breath. "I feel like we're on a movie set. Ya know, one of those historical chick flicks. Do they actually ballroom dance in here? Cuz that is *not* in my repertoire."

"Don't worry about it. No one wants to dance with you."

He smirks, looking around the room. "I've been getting *the look* from a lotta ladies here."

"You've been getting *the look* from the entire room because you're an outcast."

His chest puffs out. "Outcast only makes me more appealing. I'm forbidden fruit. Just need to apply my signature charm, and they'll be eating out of my hand."

"Keep it zipped."

"Mouth or trousers?" he quips.

"Both."

He keeps his voice low. "Might be smart. I'm not sure who I'm related to."

I stifle a groan. The ballroom does look like a movie set, or maybe a museum piece. It's a huge room with inlaid wooden floors, gold-leaf wallpaper, crystal and gold chandeliers, and frescoed ceiling paintings.

We reach the head table lined with a row of highback red velvet chairs. The center chairs are for the bride and groom. The other seats are for the king and queen and the wedding party, which are my cousins, and a woman who resembles the bride, probably her sister.

Silvia smiles sweetly at me, and I can't help but relax a little seeing her warmth. She places her hand on my shoulder and goes up on tiptoe to whisper, "Address the king and queen as your majesty."

Seriously? I grunt in acknowledgment.

I watch as she curtsies and bows her head in front of the

king and queen. How strange that she has to do that for her own brother. "King Gabriel, Queen Anna, may I present our cousin. This is Dylan Rourke. He's been a good friend to me during my stay in the US, going all the way back to my Yale days." She turns to me with a bright smile. "Seven years now, right?"

I smile back. "Right." I turn to Gabriel and wait to see what kind of reception I'll get. He slowly rises from his seat, and we're eye to eye, similar height and build. His expression is hard. Maybe he realizes that with the exile lifted I have a legitimate claim to the throne. I'm a threat to him.

I return his unblinking stare.

His wife, Anna, stands and points at my jaw. "You remind me so much of Gabriel with your jaw tight like that." She glances at her husband. "This is exactly how you look when you're stressed or irritated."

I work on loosening my jaw because I'm not stressed or irritated. I just know better than to show weakness when facing off with another guy.

Anna elbows him in the side. He shoots her a hard look before offering his hand to me. "Welcome to Villroy, cousin."

I return his firm handshake. "Thanks." I can't force out the *your majesty*. It's just too high and mighty. He's not above me. We're equals. Family.

Anna shakes my hand too. She's young with long dark brown curly hair and sparkling brown eyes. "This reunion has been a long time coming. The Rourkes are stronger together, and it was well past time to mend the rift between the families." She beams a smile at me and then Gabriel. He gives her an indulgent smile.

I don't smile because we all know who's to blame for the rift—their family. Then I remind myself of my purpose here—peacemaker—and nod once.

Now that I've seen this place, I can only imagine the culture shock my dad went through. No servants to see to his every need, no gilt and glitter. Just a working-class lifestyle trying to provide for his growing family. My uncle hired him to do the books for his construction company, and my dad worked his ass off to learn everything he could about construction. No wonder he's bitter. They could at least have given him an allowance. Some kind of cushion.

"We need to talk to you later," Anna says. "After they cut the cake, come find us again."

I stiffen, instantly wary. Talk about what? I'm the one who has an agenda. What could they possibly want from me? Sure, Anna is all smiles, but Gabriel is not exactly warm. They'll get me alone and eliminate the threat. It's classic good cop/bad cop. Maybe I'm being paranoid, but these are extreme circumstances.

I nod to Anna and shift down the line to introduce myself to the rest of my cousins. I can hear Silvia doing the big king and queen introduction behind me to my brothers. My cousins—four princes and a princess—are polite, but seem uptight. I'm sure they can't help it, being royalty. Dad says there's a bunch of royal protocol he used to have to follow. Silvia is the exception, probably because she's the youngest and spent so much time in the US.

I meet the former queen last, the woman who took my mother's place to rule the kingdom as queen. She stands regally as though she still wears a crown, though she stepped down as queen when her husband died. She's probably in her fifties, like my own mother, her dark brown hair in a bun, her expression pleasant. "Hello, I'm Alexandra, and I want to thank you for coming. My late husband hoped for a reconciliation."

I don't know what to say. Her husband, the uncle I never met, died at only fifty-four. My dad felt terrible about ignoring his brother's repeated invitations to visit when his brother was at the end of his life. I thought his brother could've mentioned he was dying and gotten different results, but apparently his disease had to be kept under wraps. What do I know about the strict code of a king?

Finally I say, "Sorry you just got us."

"No need to be sorry. It was a difficult situation for all." Her eyes shine with unshed tears, and she swallows visibly. "I was part of an arranged marriage to the future king of Villroy.

When your father abdicated, I married his brother in his place. Please pass along a thank-you to your father for giving me my husband." She blinks tears away. "We were very close."

I shift on the heels of my dress shoes, uncomfortable with her tears and also surprised she's sending my dad a thank-you. He was forced to abdicate the throne in order to marry my mother, a commoner. It was a huge scandal at the time. Never been done in the history of the kingdom. I thought everyone here was furious that my dad abdicated. Why else would they have been so harsh in his punishment? He was exiled with nothing but the shirt on his back.

"Sure, I'll pass along the message," I say.

She smiles. "Thank you. It looks like you come from a large family like ours. Are you close?"

"Yeah." I look down the line at my knucklehead brothers on their best behavior in their tuxes and smile. "They turned out all right." We all work at my uncle's company, Byrne Construction, so we're always in each other's faces.

After the introductions, a servant shows us to our table, where we have a formal dinner with fancy china bearing the royal crest—a lion wearing a crown with the sea and a fish beneath. I recognize it from online research. When I was a kid, it used to give me a lift on a crap day to know I was secretly royal. Try telling your Brooklyn pal that you're really a prince if you'd like a punch in the mouth. My brothers and I kept it close to our chests, but we stood taller, knowing it.

A continuous parade of servants weaves through the ball-room, bearing covered silver dishes. The food is all fancy gourmet stuff like they serve at those foodie restaurants—caviar, seared tuna with seaweed salad, lobster, truffle mashed potatoes. I only know the specifics because the servant announces each dish before he lifts the lid with a flourish. I can only imagine the exorbitant cost for this recep-tion with all the people here. There's gotta be at least a hundred people chowing down.

When we finish eating, the band plays a waltz for the bride and groom. They look like something out of a movie the way they dance, gazing into each other's eyes. Sean raises an eyebrow at me. *Yeah, yeah, ballroom dance in a ballroom.* I guess you get forced into dance lessons when you're royal. Glad I got to play sports instead. More waltzes follow as the bridal party joins in and then everyone else. We just sit back and watch. I consider taking a walk outside, but it's cold and pitch-black. It's like they have a thing against streetlights here. With the palace being at the top of the hill in the center of the island, I could accidentally wander off a cliff or something.

After a while, people settle back in their seats for cake. I watch the happy couple feed each other cake, and get a twinge in my chest. I don't even know them that well, but the love between them is clear as day. I wouldn't mind having a woman look at me like that, like I'm her hero. Most women look at me with a flirty smile, which means nothing more than they're hoping for a good time. I want more than that, which is probably why I haven't pursued a woman in a while. I just got tired of the emptiness of only sharing a night or two. Like I'm some hot piece of meat, which I am, but still. I want something *real*. I grew up in a big happy family, and I always saw that for myself down the line. My parents are a great example of when it's right. Problem is, I never met the right woman.

Queen Anna stops by my table. "Dylan, could you come with me?"

I stand, feeling my brothers' eyes on me. I told them about this royal meeting just in case I don't make it back. I said it like I was joking, but the tense feeling in my gut right now says maybe it's good they know the deal. "Sure."

She gestures for me to follow her to the exit, an open archway, where Gabriel is waiting with a stone-faced guard. Nothing concerning in having a fully armed guard join us for a meeting, right? Now who's paranoid?

"I'll give you a tour on the way to the audience chamber," Anna says brightly.

Audience chamber. I'm not sure what that is, but chamber sounds ominous. Will there be an audience to watch my execution? No, they wouldn't go that far. Probably just a threat to not even *think* about making a play for the throne.

I glance at Gabriel, whose stern expression gives nothing away. Anna's cheerful demeanor is such a contrast to Gabriel's that I can't help but think good cop/bad cop is in play here.

"You saw the grand entrance hall on your way in," Anna says, gesturing in that direction. "I remember the first time I saw it, I was blown away. It's just so majestic, right?" She's not a stuffy royal at all. She's young and American. Ironic because my mother was once the young American in love with the crown prince. If the royal family had been more accepting back then, my mother could've been where Anna is right now. But then I would've had to grow up here, and that wouldn't have been fun at all. I ran wild all over the neighborhood with my brothers as a kid. I'm sure Gabriel was never allowed to run wild a day in his life.

I incline my head. "Two stories of white marble is grand all right."

She grins. "I love your Brooklyn accent. So earthy."

I glance over at Gabriel to see how he takes her observation. I'm not sure "earthy" is a compliment. His lips curve the slightest bit.

I turn to Anna. "You guys speak real proper around here, so I guess that's why I stand out as…earthy."

"It's a good thing," she says, putting a hand on my arm. "I like down-to-earth people."

We head down a long hallway with tall frosted windows and white wood paneling. More frescoes on the ceiling with intricate plaster frames overhead draw my eye. Construction on this place must've taken decades, considering the tools they had back then. I'd guess the palace is a couple of centuries old.

Anna fills me in on the kingdom, which she says was dying due to the fishing industry suffering from low fish populations. She and Gabriel preserved the Rourke legacy by shifting the fishing industry to cosmetics using stuff from the sea, which they use at the new day spa and also sell online. Adrian opened a casino to diversify their business venture. I knew about their businesses, but I didn't know how bad their economy had been. Gabriel joins in, speaking with great pride on how well everything is going now. I can't help but admire what they've accomplished. Imagine running an entire country and bringing it from the brink of collapse to thriving again. It must've taken a lot of hard work.

Anna opens a door to point out the formal dining room. I get a glimpse of a long gleaming dark wood table with a huge floral centerpiece, and another gold and crystal chandelier. The palace has a look—high-class gold—and clearly they've got a lot of it. If they don't kill me, a loan is a real possibility.

"We're heading to the west wing now," she says. "The west and east wing form the courtyard out back, which leads to the formal gardens and, ultimately, the sea. Just about all roads lead to the sea here."

"It is an island," Gabriel and I say at the same time. Weird.

Anna shivers. "Spooky. You guys could be twins, except Gabriel's a year younger. I think you would've been close as kids. I hope you can get to know each other as adults."

"I would like that very much," Gabriel says, smiling at her. Obviously he says it for Anna's benefit. He doesn't even look at me.

"Sure, we'll keep in touch," I say, also for Anna's benefit. Fact is, Gabriel's here doing his king thing, and I'm working back home. Does she really think we're gonna be best buds? *Hey, Gabe, have you tried out the new diamond turbo blade for cutting marble?* He does have plenty of marble around here. I stifle a laugh at the thought.

Anna points out a few more rooms along the way and some historic Viking stuff on the wall, shields and swords, mostly, from our ancestors before we reach the audience chamber. It's not horrific, though the antique-looking wooden double throne at the very end of the enormous room gives me pause. I swear if Gabriel and Anna sit on that throne and expect me to bow or some shit like that before they make some pronouncement that puts me in my place, I can't be held responsible for my actions. We're equals, even if we live in two different worlds.

Anna gestures me on. "Take a seat on the throne with Gabriel. I'll be right back."

Me on the throne?

I stare at it and move forward slowly, almost as if in a trance. I imagined this moment as a kid when I was pissed about something, taking my place as king and doing whatever the hell I wanted with unlimited resources at my fingertips. I never thought it would happen in real life.

"What's your life like in Brooklyn?" Gabriel asks, drawing me out of my trance.

"Can't complain."

"Silvia tells me you all work in construction. Business is good?"

"Yeah, it's all right. Slow now in the winter. We'll be busy again come spring." I give him a sideways look. "How's your life here in Villroy?"

He flashes a smile that makes his entire expression go from rigid to relaxed in an instant. "Fantastic! I have a daughter now, Mila. She's sixteen months old, walking and just starting to talk. She's the light of my life." His voice chokes with emotion, and he clears his throat. "Truly, I've never been happier."

A stab of jealousy surprises me. It's just after looking out for my five younger brothers my whole life, I've always seen myself as a dad down the line. I thought I would be by now at thirty-three. Clearly, he's thrilled about it. "Congrats on your little girl. So, uh, how do you like being king?"

He gets serious. "I do my duty. I'm lucky to have Anna as a partner. She's the one who brought the kingdom from the brink of collapse and into the next century. It was her genius idea to use our fishing industry in cosmetics manufacturing. It preserved our traditional way of life while modernizing it at the same time."

He takes a seat on the throne and gestures for me to do the same on the throne next to him. I step up the dais and ease into the seat. *Nice.* The throne could be more comfortable with the hard wood, but damn. I feel like a fucking king up here, surveying a room full of imaginary people looking to me for leadership.

"How's it feel?" he asks.

"It feels right." Strange but true.

"Do you resent me for taking your place?"

I hesitate. I don't resent him exactly, but it's hard to see him on the throne knowing it's because my dad was treated unfairly.

"You don't have to answer," he says. "An inane question. Of course you resent what you've been denied through no fault of your own. I would feel the same."

"It's just my dad, ya know? It wasn't right the way things went down."

"Agreed."

Anna approaches with a servant holding a large wooden box. "We'd like you to give this to your father. A gift that we hope he'll take as the gesture of peace it is."

My eyes widen. *A gift for my father?*

The servant sets the box in my hands. I open the metal latches, lift the lid, and my breath rushes out. It's a jeweled gold crown and scepter set on dark blue velvet. There's gotta be more than a hundred diamonds on the crown, along with sapphires, rubies, and pearls. The scepter is topped with a cross with an emerald and encrusted with diamonds and rubies. This must be worth a fortune!

I definitely can't ask Gabriel for a loan after he gave me this incredible gift. I'll tell Sean we have to find another way. Not that we've had any luck with the banks. Yet. We can try a few more.

"You should probably fly back on our jet," Anna says to me. "It'll be tough to get this home safely on a commercial flight. Imagine explaining it to security!"

"Yeah, sure." I can't stop staring at it. I've never seen so many jewels in one place. "Was this my dad's?"

"Yes," Gabriel says. "It was made for him. My father wore it only until a new set could be created for him. There was a quick succession after our grandfather died and your father abdicated. I'm told your father kept his relationship with your mother a secret until our grandfather was on his deathbed. Perhaps the shock of that revelation led to the subsequent harshness of his exile."

I tear my gaze away from the set to stare at him. "I didn't know it was a secret relationship."

"Your father was engaged to my mother," Gabriel says. "It had been arranged since they were children. My mother lived halfway around the world. They were to meet on their wedding day."

I grimace. I can't imagine marrying someone you've never met. The story I knew was that my mom, Tara Byrne, was a Brooklyn girl on a college study-abroad program in France, where she met my dad, who was visiting from nearby Villroy. Guess my grandfather wasn't in a forgiving mood as he lay dying while his son sprang the big news on him. Would things have been different if he'd told his parents about his love for my mom instead of keeping it secret until the last possible minute? Or did he always know they'd never accept a commoner, and was struggling to make the right choice for him—kingdom or love?

Anna leans close to me. "Do you want to try it on?"

I jolt. "No. This was never meant for me." The truth of that sinks in. Only royal lines on both sides would've led to me being king. Though now with the change in leadership on Villroy, that no longer matters. Gabriel and Anna's daughter, Mila, will one day be queen despite having a mother with no royal bloodlines. Timing, man.

Gabriel and Anna owe me nothing, really, yet they've given me this amazing gift. I pick up the scepter, admiring the craftsmanship of the unique piece. My dad will be so relieved to have this set back, even if it's not with the role he expected to have. This crown and scepter were rightfully his. He probably had it in hand on more than one occasion, maybe even wore it.

My voice comes out rough. "Thank you. I'm sure this will mean a lot to him."

Only when I finally get home and give it to my dad, his brows draw together, his jaw tight. I resemble him, but he's got gray at his temples now and some lines by his blue-green eyes. He says the lines are from laughing too much.

"It's meant as a peace gesture," I say.

He shoves the box back into my hands. "You keep it. You were next in line to be king. I robbed you of that. It's the least I can do."

"You didn't rob me of anything. I woulda never been king because Mom was a commoner. It's not like I woulda been here without her."

"How did they treat you and your brothers?"

"Ya know, after we spent some time with our cousins, they weren't as uptight as I first thought. It went okay." We actually had a good time, drinking and playing poker. I leave out the snubbing we got from some of the older generation. My dad has suffered enough.

"Good. Did King Gabriel agree to a loan?"

"I didn't feel right asking him after he gave us this valuable gift," I say, lifting the box in my hands.

He jabs a finger at the box. "This was mine to begin with. I—you were denied the compensation you deserved for your place in the kingdom. You should have received something greater than the return of my own possession."

"Dad, it's fine. We'll find another way." I undo the latches on the box and lift the lid, angling it so he can see.

My dad takes the crown out, admiring it from all sides. He's quiet for a moment, his expression solemn. "I remember this like it was yesterday."

"Keep it. They wanted you to have it."

He sets it on my head, surprising me. It's heavy from all the jewels. "It suits you. My son, the king." He pulls his phone from his khakis pocket and takes a picture, showing me it.

I stare at the screen for a moment. Maybe it's my resemblance to my dad, but it actually doesn't look as strange as I thought it would. *No.* This is not me; this is my father.

I take the crown off my head and set it carefully back in the box. "I was never gonna be king." I offer him the box again, and he crosses his arms, denying his gift.

I understand. Accepting the gift means forgiving his family after they cut him off. "I'll keep this in the safe at work. You'll always know where it is if you want it."

"It's yours," he insists.

I shake my head. I know my place. I'm key to my uncle's construction company. I've managed the crew for years, and I've been taking a larger role in running the business too, working side by side with my uncle. Sean and I will figure out a way to get into real estate too. This is my life. There is no circumstance where I will ever be asked to step up as king. I'm half commoner, the rogue prince.

And no one gives a shit about my royal blood here in Brooklyn.

2

Ariana

Ooh, there he is, Dylan Rourke, the secret prince. What a crock! I bet he made that up just to get into girls' pants. I struggle with the key at the door of my parents' house, balancing grocery bags, and studiously ignore his stare from the stoop approximately six feet away. We grew up in adjoining brick rowhouses. He's standing there in a black leather motorcycle jacket and faded jeans, holding a wooden box and, dammit, even after all these years, he still looks disgustingly gorgeous. It must be the bone structure with the high cheekbones and square jaw. Or maybe it's his thick dark brown hair, blue eyes, scruff, and a hard body shaped by years of construction work. Tall, muscled, badass. Like I care.

I finally get the stupid door unlocked and sail inside, over-heated purely from the battle with the door. "Ma, I got the groceries!"

No response. She must've gone for a walk with my dad. We're having above-freezing temps here in what's typically a frigid New York winter. "Practically spring!" Ma said earlier, though it's New Year's Day.

I head for the kitchen in back, set the bags on the counter, and drape my down jacket over the back of a chair. I haven't seen Dylan since I left for college at eighteen. Growing up,

Dylan used to tease me relentlessly, tugging my pigtails and calling me "Airy Fairy," probably because I used to wear tutus and dance all the time. My friends call me Air, short for Ariana. Anyway, I loved ballet and dreamed of dancing in the New York City Ballet at Lincoln Center. Then, seemingly overnight, my body burst into curves—big boobs, hips, butt. I was no longer the ideal dancer shape and was passed over for the major parts at my dance company. I worked harder, pushed myself beyond what I'd ever attempted before, with the strain, sore muscles, and exhaustion to show for it. Finally, my instructor had a frank talk with me about the nonexistence of my future career and, at fifteen, I quit. Devastated.

My mom, practical as she is, told me to use my brain and focus on my education, so I did. I went to Stanford, majored in communications, and worked as the marketing manager for my husband's family firm, a real estate development company in San Francisco. We recently divorced after eight years of marriage, but I kept working there since it had all been on amicable terms. I truly loved him and maybe I wasn't ready to let him go. We started out agreeing on no kids, and then, when I got older, I realized I wanted them. The divorce was his idea since he was never going to change his mind on the kid issue. A hard blow, but I told myself people change, and this was the right choice for both of us. I didn't even take half his assets, though I could have under California law. I took only what I'd contributed to the marriage. The house was a gift from his parents, so that stayed with him. No alimony. I'm an independent woman. It was so very civilized. I really thought I was okay with everything, but then only six months after the divorce, he showed up at work with his girlfriend, a pretty young blonde, and—

She's pregnant. Eight months pregnant.

Twist the knife, thanks! The man who swore he never wanted to have kids stood there introducing me to his new love and their soon-to-be baby, which obviously happened while we were still married, and he was so fucking *happy* about it. He just didn't want to have kids with me. He didn't love me the way I loved him. My throat tightens painfully at the memory. I swallow hard and focus on putting away the groceries, my eyes hot.

I quit my job under the circumstances, so here I am back at my parents' house, unemployed and trying to move forward with the next phase of my life. This is my do-over. Soon I'll have a new life, new job, and, hopefully in the not-too-distant future, a new baby. It's part of the reason I moved back to Brooklyn. I want to have family nearby for support. In fact, I've already chosen the perfect donor from a sperm bank. He's got fantastic genes—tall, a former lacrosse player, no inheritable health issues, and a PhD in anthropology. We're even the same blood type, so the child would match me. As soon as I get all the pieces of my life in place, I'm making the insemination appointment. Just thinking about it brings me some peace. My ex kept me from my dream of motherhood for years, but now no one can stop me. Not even my well-meaning, but overly concerned mother.

She went ballistic when I told her about my sperm donor. She insisted she'd have to get in touch with the father and his family. Like that's normal. I exhale sharply. I made the hard choices—starting over out here—because this is important to me. I'm thirty-one and more than ready to be a mom.

Step one, a good job. Maybe I'll start my own real estate development company. I have the experience, and the property values are skyrocketing here in Brooklyn. My parents' neighborhood, Windsor Terrace, has seen a real bump in housing values. More people want to settle here for the schools and small-town feel with its tree-lined streets, well-maintained homes, and low traffic volume. A lot of Brooklyn neighborhoods are going up in value. Only problem is, I don't have the money to invest. My future planning is interrupted by the roar of a Harley motorcycle out front. Dylan. Did he manage to strap that box onto the back of his bike? I'm not going to peek out the window.

His teasing voice plays in my memory. *Where's your tutu, Airy Fairy?*

It was Dylan's favorite question for me after I stopped wearing them at ten. He wouldn't shut up about it and, once I quit ballet, the reminder hurt. I used to glare at him, shouting on the inside, "It's buried like my dreams!" I was on the shy side as a kid, or I would've cussed him out.

I finish with the groceries, help myself to a glass of water, and sink into a vinyl kitchen chair. Unfortunately, I've thought about Dylan a lot over the years, both good and bad, which is why I avoid him. The man is burned into my brain. My mind goes back to that fateful day. Me, young and stupid. Him, young and cocky.

It was a sunny Saturday in August, the day before my big trip out to California for college, and I was determined to lose my virginity before I left. I figured college would be more fun if I'd gotten past that awkwardness. God, I thought I was so smart thinking ahead like that. In fact, I'd planned it for weeks. I knew when my parents were going to be away in New Jersey, helping my older sister, Rosalie, move into her new apartment for her first job. I deliberately procrastinated on packing my stuff for college so I wouldn't have to go with them. I had the house to myself. Now I just needed the guy. I thought long and hard about that. I needed someone I wouldn't mind leaving, and the guy had to be at least a little bit good at it so it wouldn't be a horrible experience. Dylan, at twenty, was whispered about by the neighborhood girls as being "good to get with." Add to that our mutual parents' feud, and it lent a delicious sense of rebellion to choosing him. (Long story, but the feud is not my family's fault. If his mother can't keep track of her serving spoons, that's her problem. My mother is not a thief.) With our parents' well-known animosity, no one would ever believe I'd been with him. Perfect plan. Not.

He roared up on his Harley, everyone could hear that thing, and my virgin heart pounded.

I peeked out the front window. Yup, it was him. I burst out the front door, rushed down the steps, and stood in front of him on the sidewalk. He looked like his usual badass cocky self as he got off his bike with his black helmet, tight blue T-shirt, and jeans molded to his powerful thighs.

I made my move. "Hi."

He took off his helmet, his dark brown hair sexily rumpled. He was tall, at least six feet, with wide shoulders and bulging biceps I was newly appreciating. "Hey, Airy Fairy, wh—"

I cut him off before he could ask me about my damn tutu. "I heard you're a prince." As opening lines, it was a good one because I had the perfect follow-up: *I always wanted to be with a prince.* I waited, adrenaline firing through me.

He stared at me.

"Sean told me." His brother Sean and I were in the same grade in school.

"Sean lies."

I leaned close, surprised to find he actually smelled good. Really good. Like fresh air and man. "I have the house to myself," I whispered.

He stared at me again, but this time there was a spark in his blue eyes. Was he interested? It was hard to tell. His eyes stayed on my face despite the fact that I wore a yellow floral minidress with thin straps and a fitted bodice that showed off my cleavage.

I hitched a thumb toward my house. "My parents are helping Rosalie move into her new place in Jersey. It should take a while. You wanna come inside?" *Ooh! I made a double entendre. Look at me, flirting so awesome!*

His head slowly tilted to the side. "For what?"

Maybe not so awesome at this flirting thing.

I gathered my courage and placed a hand on his chest. The heat of him burned through the thin fabric of his T-shirt, and my entire body flushed hot. I risked a glance up at him. He stared at my hand on his chest. I took it as a good sign that he didn't immediately push my hand away. Still, I dropped it just in case he wasn't cool with it. I wasn't sure we were on the same page.

"You should come over," I said in a light flirty voice. "We could spend some time together just us."

He stared at me for a long moment, and my hopes rose. It seemed he got my message and was giving it serious consideration. "Yeah, uh, no, thanks." He turned and strode up the front stoop of his house next door.

I huffed and followed him up the steps. "Why not?"

He looked down at me, his gaze dropping briefly to my cleavage and jerking back to my eyes. "You hate me."

"I don't hate you." *I just find you irritating and way too cocky.*

"You think you're better than me."

My glares must've been more withering than I'd realized. Still, I'd thought guys loved the chance to have sex.

Running out of time here!

Desperation tinged my voice. "I need to get rid of it before college, and I leave tomorrow."

One corner of his mouth lifted. "What's 'it' exactly?"

My cheeks flamed, but I choked out the words. "My virginity."

He smirked. "Just wanted to hear ya say it. Now ask some other guy."

My lips pressed together. He knew what I meant, and he made me say the embarrassing thing out loud. The fact that he was irritating was, unfortunately, not a deterrent. I'd known that my entire life. I also knew I was not going through all this again with another guy, and he was still ideal, being both gorgeous and experienced.

I was on a mission.

I pressed on. "I'm asking *you.*"

"Why?"

I hadn't expected to need a reason. I fumbled for a good one after years of his teasing and years of me glaring, and our families being on the outs. "Cuz I know you, and—" oh, I hated to admit it, but this was an urgent situation "—and you're cute."

He frowned. "Cute. Puppies are cute."

"Okay, you're handsome!"

He gave me a wicked smile that made my heart thump harder. "Sexy."

I rolled my eyes, but my heart was racing. "Fine. That too."

He pinched my chin, lifting my face to his. "What's the catch?"

I gulped. "No catch. No strings. I'm leaving tomorrow."

His eyes burned into mine, and sparks skittered across my skin. His voice was low and husky. "Kiss me, and I'll think it over."

We were on his front stoop. Any of the neighbors could see us. This was a tight-knit neighborhood that went back generations, which meant I was sure this would get back to my parents. "Can we go somewhere more private?"

"No."

I hesitated.

He dropped his hold on me. "Go home, Ariana."

My jaw went slack. He actually said my name. He never said my real name, not even my nickname Air. Always with the stupid Airy Fairy.

He stuck his key in the door, and I realized I was losing him. I grabbed his forearm to stop him, the heat of his skin bringing a delicious warmth.

He slanted a sideways look at me. "Yeah?"

"Okay. I'll kiss you here."

"Forget it."

I was so irritated by how difficult he was making this for me that I grabbed his head, pulled him down to me, and kissed him hard. He didn't touch me, didn't kiss me back, and I gentled the kiss, hoping he liked that better. Suddenly he was kissing me back, his mouth sealing over mine. A rush of heat, a sigh, and I melted against him. He was that good.

He broke the kiss abruptly. "Alright, let's go." He took my hand and walked down the steps of his house and up the steps of mine. I was so excited I forgot I was going to sneak him in through the back.

I was nervous when we got to my bedroom, especially when he immediately zoomed in on the condom I left on top of the nightstand for this well-planned event.

He set his motorcycle helmet on the floor by the door; then he shut the door and locked it. The click of the lock sounded loud and ominous. My pulse raced. I was alone with Dylan

Rourke in my bedroom. My conquest, who I now feared had the upper hand. He was big, powerful with muscles from his construction work, and I'd offered an invitation I wasn't sure I could take back.

Maybe he sensed my nerves because he took my hand and pulled me toward him in a slow confident way, all the way into his arms, before kissing me like he had all day. Deep, hot, wet kisses that made my limbs heavy, my body hot, my mind blessedly blank. By the time he guided me to the bed, I was ready to strip naked. Instead he stretched out next to me, fully dressed, and kissed me more. His hands were big and calloused, but he touched me gently, cupping my jaw, stroking my throat, tracing my collarbone, sliding down my bare shoulder. My skin tingled everywhere he touched.

He kissed me for so long, my chin got whisker burn, and I swore my lips were swollen. I broke the kiss. "I'm ready."

I started to unbutton the small buttons on the bodice of my dress, but he brushed my hands away and did it himself. Slowly. Kissing every inch of exposed skin. I was in a fever of hot need, my fingers raking through his hair, half dazed by the most intense experience of my life. This was nothing like the make-out sessions I'd had with other guys. His rep was so well deserved.

By the time we were both naked, I was more than ready. He was so gorgeous, tanned and muscular, the sexiest man I'd ever seen. I spread my legs and pulled him toward me.

He kissed me again, long and deep, like he couldn't get enough. I was consumed by desire. I never knew it could be like this.

He lifted his head. "Lemme try somethin' out on ya."

Try something out?

My throat went dry. "Can't we just do it the regular way?"

"Yeah, we will, but I wanna try somethin' first."

My eyes narrowed, my desire cooling rapidly. "Where'd ya learn it from, another girl?"

He cupped my cheek and kissed me, just a brush of his lips that warmed me. "From a book. You like books."

"You read a sex book?"

"Yeah. It's supposed to feel real good for the girl. Hey, you don't like it, I'll stop. Don't worry, it's perfectly normal."

I studied him for a long moment, and he gave me a sexy smile, his blue eyes sparkling. In that moment I trusted him. After all, he hadn't leapt at me or ripped my clothes off. He'd kissed me for so long my lips were swollen.

"Okay," I said.

He grinned. "Thanks. Tell me if ya like it."

And then he lowered himself down my body and kissed me. *There.* Where no one had ever kissed me before. I gasped, and then—

It. Was. Insanely. Good.

I died and came back to life. I may have called him a god.

"I liked it," I told him after, trying to catch my breath.

He nuzzled my inner thigh, a low chuckle rumbling through his chest. "Yeah, got that." He reached to the night-stand for the condom, ripped the packet open, rolled it on, and covered me with his body. "Ready?"

My lips curved in a lazy smile. He was so freaking awesome. "Ready."

His eyes burned into mine as he guided himself in. A brief flash of pain made my breath catch, and then there was an incredible ache as he filled me.

He stilled, stroking my hair back and cupping the side of my face in one large hand. I closed my eyes, telling myself to relax, it would all be over soon. And then he kissed me again in his drugging way, and I lost myself in the moment, relaxing under him as I roamed my palms over the powerful muscles of his back.

He started to move, pumping in and out, and I liked it now.

"I'm so glad you're my first," I blurted.

Our gazes locked, something deeper passing between us that only grew with feeling, like our souls were merging along with our bodies. I could barely catch my breath as lust and a sudden rush of love overwhelmed me. Time ceased to exist. Pleasure built inside me again, a tight spiral that made my nails dig into his shoulders. It built and built and then his mouth slammed over mine, and I went over, a starburst of pleasure rocking me.

His head reared back, the cords in his neck tight, and he let go with a low guttural sound.

Unbelievably amazing!

I smiled, stroking his heated shoulders and back. I was so happy, so relaxed, so *surprised*. A good surprise. Who knew I would ever have so much feeling for Dylan Rourke? The irritating, cocky guy living in enemy territory.

Suddenly he stood by the side of the bed, and I went cold.

He yanked his clothes on without a word, his back to me.

I propped up on my elbows, hardly believing what I was seeing. I finally found my voice and it sounded small. "You're leaving?"

He was dressed now, socks and shoes in hand, his gaze somewhere past my shoulder. "Good luck in college," he muttered before bolting out the door.

I stared at his helmet still on the floor by the door. In such a hurry he forgot his helmet. And he couldn't even stay long enough to put his socks and shoes on!

I raced after him with the helmet, so furious I didn't even care that I was naked. I got to the top of the stairs just as he stepped out the front door. "Have a nice life, asshole!" I yelled at the top of my lungs.

Whatta pig! I would *never* forgive him.

Enough Dylan Rourke! It's been *years*. It's being home again that's bringing this all back so vividly. Seeing him next door.

Ah, hell. Truth? He ruined me for other men. No one could compare. He haunted my dreams—his blue eyes burning into mine, his calloused hands so gentle, the heat and glory of my first taste of passion. I'd wake aching and hot and then curse him.

And wouldn't he get an even bigger head if he knew that? All those disappointing guys until I met my husband, the first guy to take his time with me the way Dylan did. And look how that turned out.

I rise from my parents' kitchen table. Dylan doesn't get

my headspace anymore. He's a pig. And I've got much more important things to think about. Like getting my life in order for my soon-to-be baby.

I grab a tumbler from the cabinet, reach behind the pasta containers for my dad's stash of whiskey, and pour myself a generous amount. Water isn't going to cut it when it comes to forgetting Dylan.

3

———

Dylan

It's the day after New Year's, and I'm back at my parents' house because they called a family meeting. It's late afternoon, which means Mom will probably have dinner at the ready too. I'm always up for a home-cooked meal, but this family meeting has me on edge. I turn off my bike, take off my helmet, and just sit there, staring at the blue front door with a growing sense of dread. We haven't had a family meeting in a long time, and my dad wouldn't share any details. Last time we had one, it was because Uncle Pat had a health scare. He's fine now.

Jesus. I hope it's not that. I don't know what I'll do if I find out the cancer is back. Uncle Pat, the owner of Byrne Construction where we all work, has been like a second father to me and my brothers. He's the one who taught us all the stuff my dad couldn't on account of his royal upbringing. Like how to use tools, how to pitch a fastball and a change-up, how to grill. My dad taught us tons of stuff too, most importantly, to take risks and be bold because we've got only one go-round in this life. Mom was all about kindness. The woman is a saint. At least it seems that way dealing with six rambunctious boys wreaking havoc at home, school, and, basically, everywhere.

What if it's something wrong with one of my parents?

I swallow hard and look away, my eye catching on the quick drop of a curtain in the front window of the Bianchis' house next door. Probably Mrs. Bianchi looking for some gossip about the Rourkes. Certainly wouldn't be Ariana spying on me. She gave me the cold shoulder yesterday. What's she doing home anyway? She hasn't been home since she married that guy out in California right after college graduation. I ignore the familiar dull ache in my chest whenever I think of her, which is more than I'll ever admit. The thing is, I never got the chance to see what might have been. That one time we were together was *intense*. I still can't wrap my head around how it was so good. She was a virgin, for crying out loud. And it was so far beyond my usual hookups, so satisfying, so damn emotional, her big brown eyes gazing into mine with a deep affection that felt like...love. Ridiculous. She couldn't have loved me. I don't know what the hell that was, which is probably why I fucked up the moment it was over.

I get off my bike. Rourkes and Bianchis don't mix. I should've known better than to take her up on her offer back then. It's brought me nothing but a damn inconvenient standard, which no woman has lived up to. I suspect she told her parents something about that day, because they've been giving me the stink eye ever since. More than just for being a Rourke, I mean.

Enough stalling. I stride up the front stoop. Family meeting time.

"There he is, Miss A-mer-i-ca!" a deep voice sings behind me.

I turn to my brother Sean and flip him the bird. He's been giving me shit about the crown Anna gave me for Dad, saying it's my tiara. "Ass."

He heads up the steps. His dark scruff is thick, nearly beard territory. "Any clue what this is about?"

"No. When ya gonna shave?"

"I need it to keep me warm." He crosses his arms in his black wool coat and fakes a shiver. When he's not at work, he dresses nice all the fucking time because he used to date this uppity woman. They lived together in her pricey neighborhood. She transformed his wardrobe, turning him into "a gentleman." Her words. They broke up, but he's been renovating her place in exchange for free rent while she starts her new life living with her Wall Street guy in the city. All very civilized. Me? I would've moved out and found my own place. I don't care if she says it was an affair of the heart not the body. It's still cheating.

I pat his cheek like a slap. "You're just too lazy to shave."

He knocks my hand away. "You think it's about Uncle Pat?"

"I hope not."

I ring the bell even though I have the key. You only need to walk in on your parents naked in the living room *once* to learn that lesson the hard way. *Shudder.* I wanted to wash my eyes out with bleach. Some things you can never unsee.

The door opens to Mom smiling at us, her blue eyes lighting up. She's got long dark brown hair, no gray showing, her fair skin smooth. People who don't know her are surprised to hear she's in her fifties. She did a bit of modeling in her teens, which she says she didn't like, but the money was good and put her through college.

"Come in!" she exclaims, stepping back from the door. "You can relax. Nobody's dying."

How did she know?

I lean down to kiss her cheek, and she hugs me. "I saw that tight jaw," she whispers.

I straighten. "I didn't know I had a tell."

She hugs Sean and smiles at me over his shoulder. "You all have tells. Mothers know."

We head into the living room. The house is turn of the century, but we've renovated it. It's one of those classic twenty-by-fifty-foot rowhouses with ten-foot-high ceilings, original oak parquet floors, and crown molding. My parents leave the pocket doors separating the living room from the kitchen and dining room permanently open. The living room is in front, large kitchen in the center with a long island and stools, and in back is a dining room table. The kitchen is the center of all activity, especially growing up in a family of eight. You want quiet? Go somewhere else. There's three bedrooms upstairs and one tucked into the basement, which is also the man cave with a Ping-Pong table and a pool table. Sean and I got the basement bedroom because we were the oldest.

Mom heads straight to the refrigerator. "Beer, iced tea, or water?"

"Beer, please," I say.

"You have to ask?" Sean asks with a grin.

Mom pulls two bottles of beer from the fridge. "I don't assume. Sometimes you're on a health kick to keep from growing a gut." She opens them with a bottle opener, sneaking a peek at our guts as she hands us each a beer.

I lift the bottom of my long-sleeved black shirt for her inspection. "Think I can deal with one beer?" I've got abs of steel.

She waves a hand airily. "I wasn't judging. Drink what you want." She leans toward the doorway leading to the basement. "Daniel, your favorite sons are here!"

Sean and I exchange a grin. I point to myself. Dad calls all of us his favorite sons. One thing I've always known—our dad is proud of us. He never heard that kind of thing from his own father growing up and made it a point to let us know.

Dad appears a few minutes later. "You bellowed?"

"You can't hear me down there in your man cave," Mom says. "Talk to your sons, but not about *that*."

Dad wraps an arm around her shoulders, pulls her in, and plants a kiss on her lips. "Your command is my wish."

She looks into his eyes with a smile. "That's backwards, honey, but I like it anyway."

They gaze into each other's eyes, smiling, until the doorbell rings and Mom pulls away to answer it.

Dad rubs his clean-shaven jaw. "How're you two doing?"

"We two are great," Sean says. "What's up with the family meeting?"

Dad looks toward the door. "Your uncle will explain." He heads out to join Mom.

I take a seat on a white-cushioned island stool and peer into the living room. Uncle Pat is holding a briefcase. Hmm… maybe we're here for work stuff.

"Just two of ya?" he booms, striding into the kitchen. He's nine years older than Mom at sixty-seven with short silver hair, a matching beard, and sharp blue eyes. He sets his briefcase down, leaning against the island.

"The important ones are here," I say.

He laughs and claps me on the shoulder. "Uncle tax," he says, taking a sip of my beer.

"Aunt Marian still keeping you on a diet?" I ask.

He pats his gut. "It's not working, is it?"

"Cuz you sneak," Sean says. "I saw ya with the drawer of mini Snickers."

Uncle Pat lifts his palms. "Great, now everyone knows. That drawer is as good as empty."

My brothers filter in—Jack, Connor, Brendan, and Garrett —helping themselves to beers. We all resemble my dad, except most of us have our mom's blue eyes. Everyone in the neighborhood can spot a Rourke son. We've got his build, six feet and change for a few of my brothers, wide shoulders, sharp cheekbones, square jaw. My brothers and I have varying degrees of scruff. Mine's probably the cleanest since I shaved recently.

Mom puts out a large bowl of tortilla chips, a bowl of guacamole, and a plate with sliced salami, pepperoni, cheese, and crackers. It's cheerful chaos, except I keep thinking about why the hell we're here. Uncle Pat is having too good a time joking around with everyone for it to be bad news. What is it? Did we get a big contract for spring?

His wife, Aunt Marian, arrives, giving us all kisses on the cheek before going over to talk to Mom. Okay, so maybe this is a couple announcement? Maybe Uncle Pat and Aunt Marian are going to be grandparents again. Their daughter lives in Seattle.

Finally, I can't take the suspense anymore. I pitch my voice over the noise. "Uncle Pat, what's the news? Why're we all here?"

Dad clinks a fork against his glass a few times. "I hereby call this family meeting to order."

We go silent, all eyes on Dad.

Dad turns to Mom. "Shall we review the minutes from the previous meeting?"

Mom bites back a smile. "From seven years ago? Let me think."

I cup my hands over my mouth. "Boo-oo-oo."

"You're out of order, sir!" Dad exclaims. "To the dungeon!" He jabs a finger toward the basement stairs.

I shake my head. Sometimes his royal side comes out at the strangest times. "Uncle Pat, please, what's going on?"

My uncle grins and takes us all in. "Big news."

Silence.

No one drags out a story for maximum entertainment value better than my uncle. Take him into an Irish bar and he'll hold court with a rapt audience for hours.

I fake strangle him, and everyone laughs.

My uncle stands and spreads his arms wide. "The big news is I'm retiring!"

My parents and aunt clap for him. My brothers stare in shock. Me, I'm thinking who's going to run the shop? It's Byrne Construction and he's been running it for more than forty years. Will I get to run it since I'm the most experienced and the crew chief, or is he going to divide it among me and my brothers, or worse, shut the business down?

"When?" I ask.

"Now," he says, smiling like a maniac, his blue eyes twinkling. He helps himself to a long swallow of Sean's beer. Aunt Marian barely twitches at the sight.

"Now?" I echo incredulously. "You can't just retire now."

"I sure can," he says with a laugh. "New year, new me. Marian and I rented an RV. We're going to drive down to Florida and look for the perfect spot to spend our twilight years."

"What the fuck are twilight years?" Garrett asks and, at Mom's glare, corrects himself. "I meant what the hell —err, frig."

Everyone starts talking at once, firing questions at my uncle, who gave no indication before this major announcement that he had any intention of taking off to Florida in an RV for whatever the hell they do down there in Florida.

"Everybody shut up!" I bark.

"You shut up," one of my brothers says. I don't bother to look at who said it because my eyes are locked on Uncle Pat.

"What happens to Byrne Construction?" I ask.

His eyes mist over as he looks at me. I'm instantly wary. He crosses behind where I'm sitting and puts both hands on my shoulders. "Everyone, you're looking at the new CEO of Byrne Construction. I'm signing the business over to be co-owned by each of my fine Rourke nephews, with Dylan overseeing it. He's the oldest and most experienced. My right-hand man."

I'm frozen in place. Shock doesn't begin to cover it. I had no idea he wanted to retire let alone hand the business over to us. I glance around at my brothers to see if they mind that I'm their boss now.

"Guess it pays to be firstborn," Sean mutters.

I've inherited the kingdom, except it's a construction company I've been working for since I was sixteen years old. I should be happy, but instead all I feel is the crushing responsibility of taking a company my uncle has successfully run for the last forty years and keeping it going. I can't let him down. It has to succeed.

All those jobs depend on me.

My brothers' fates tied to my decisions.

All of it on my shoulders.

Why did he have to spring it on me like this?

Uncle Pat is the one with all the connections. I don't have nearly his network just from the few years I've worked on the business side. He's the one who brings in new business. I step in after the project is ours. Shit. I'm not ready for this. You need a constant supply of new business to keep going. No new projects, no one gets paid.

I look over my shoulder at my uncle. "I need you to stick around, show me the ins and outs."

"Just say thank you."

"Thank you, but—"

"Let's celebrate!" he exclaims. "Bring out the cake, Tara!"

Mom pulls a sheet cake from the refrigerator. "I got the kind with the strawberry filling you like."

"From Mona's Bakery, right?" Uncle Pat asks.

Mom sets it on the center of the island. "Of course. I know what you like." She gestures for him to stand next to her and wraps an arm around his waist. "Congratulations!" She gestures for us to all join in.

Everyone follows suit, dutifully congratulating him while Uncle Pat and Aunt Marian grin like loons. Obviously they've been planning this awhile. The white cake says in blue icing: Enjoy Retirement, Pat! Would've been nice if I'd been clued in at least as long as the bakery.

It occurs to me that we'll still have Dad, who does the financial side. "Dad, you're sticking around, right?"

He looks to Mom, who gives him a bright smile.

Fuck. He's leaving too? He's not old enough to retire, is he? He's only fifty-eight.

Dad stands tall, shoulders back in his regal way. "Since Pat's retiring and he's passing on leadership, I'm going to move on too."

My jaw clenches. "What does that mean?"

Mom goes to him, and he wraps an arm around her shoulders. *Please tell me they're not renting an RV to live out their twilight years in Florida.*

The room goes quiet, all eyes on my parents.

A muscle ticks in my jaw. I'd like to be happy about my good fortune. If only it wasn't being dumped on me without any backup. What if it goes bankrupt on my watch?

"I've decided to start a new career," Dad says.

At fifty-eight? I nearly put my head down on the island counter and groan. I'm tempted to bang it a few times too.

"As King of Brooklyn?" Sean quips.

I throw a slice of salami at his head. Various food items fly through the air, all aimed at him.

"Cut the food fight," Mom snaps while serving up slices of retirement cake.

"What?" Sean asks, picking bits of meat and cheese out of his hair and brushing crumbs from his shirt. "Dad could be King of Brooklyn. He's got the crown now."

"I'm taking a real estate course," Dad says. "I like meeting new people, and it'll get me out from behind a desk. I thought we could work together—Byrne Construction and Rourke Realty." He looks to me. "You and Sean have been wanting to get into real estate. If only you'd asked for what you were rightfully denied in Villroy—"

"I told ya we'd find another way," I say.

His jaw clenches tight, his lips in a flat line. He takes it personally, the fact that I don't have what he thinks I deserve. Probably because it's what *he* really deserved, and he regrets not having it to pass on to the next generation. He was raised on royal traditions related to inheritance. Finally, he recovers himself and says, "In any case, if you all build or renovate a property, I could help find people to buy or rent."

"Thanks. Great idea." My mind latches on to this new piece. Dad knew we'd get the company soon, which must be why he was so keen on us getting funding through our royal cousins. He knew I could use it to expand into real estate development in a big way, much bigger than flipping houses on the weekend. Investing in land, building new, rebuilding an entire area. Only what do I know about real estate market analysis? This is much more complicated than finding the worst house in a good neighborhood to renovate. How do you get top dollar, or even decide what to build? Condo, office space, apartment complex—

I stand abruptly, muttering, "I need some fresh air."

"Wait, I'll go with you," Uncle Pat says.

I hold up a palm. "I'll be back soon." I need to clear my head. I'm in the deep end of a rough sea with no life preserver.

I stride out the door and the cold air hits me. I left my jacket behind, but there's no way I'm going back for it. I need to move. I head down the stairs and stride down the sidewalk toward Prospect Park. Later, I'll sit my uncle and dad down to wring every bit of information I can get out of them. Now I need to get my head on straight.

I get to the park and start at a jog down the trail. The sun's starting to set, and the park is clearing out. I speed up. Before I know it, I'm running full speed along the loop. It's a little over three miles, and I make it around once before a cramp in my side has me bending over.

"Someone's getting old," a feminine voice teases.

4

____

Dylan

I straighten, holding my side. Well, if it isn't my mortal enemy—Ariana Bianchi. Just the person I want to witness my manly breakdown. She's in a bright pink hoodie with black yoga pants that cling to her shapely legs. As kids, she was nearly always head to toe in pink or something with glitter. She used to catch my eye with her glossy dark brown hair in a bun, whirling and twirling in ballerina tutus like the neighborhood was her stage. Her nickname was Air, but I called her Airy Fairy because she was such a girly girl who never got dirty, except that one time. Do *not* think about that now.

I search my beleaguered brain for a comeback. "Aren't you too old to wear a pigtail?" I gesture to her hair up in a high pigtail.

"It's called a ponytail and fuck you."

I stare at her mouth, surprised at her language. My memory of her is of a quiet girl twirling or, later, always with her nose in a book. She did curse at me once, on the way out the door back when—nope. Not going there. Her lips are the same pink as her hoodie, and the lower lip is fuller. *Sexy.*

I jerk my head up. "They teach you to curse at your fancy college?"

"The Rourkes taught me to curse. That's all I used to hear next door—F this, F that."

"F that." I laugh, surprising myself.

Her brown eyes dance with amusement. "That's right. F that."

We crack up. I think I'm losing it.

She pulls her ankle up behind her, stretching. "I saw you running like a pack of wolves was chasing you. What's got your pants on fire?"

I laugh again. "Were you this funny when we were kids?"

She stretches her other leg. "Musta been. You were too busy teasing to ever talk to me."

The cramp in my side eases. "Did you really *want* to talk to me?"

"No."

I lift a palm in a gesture of *there you go*.

"Welp, as always, it's been bizarre. I gotta run." She takes off on the loop I just did, her high ponytail bouncing.

I look toward home and think of the crowd there celebrating something I'm not ready to celebrate. Then I look back toward the distraction of pink, who actually made me laugh in the middle of my crisis.

I jog after her and catch up, running alongside her. "Hey."

She does a double take. "You again? What gives?"

"What're you doing back home?"

"Can't I visit my parents?"

"You could, but don't they usually go out to see you in California?"

A beat passes before she says, "Yeah, well, I don't live there anymore."

"Why?"

She huffs and speeds up. I keep up with her. "Why do you care?" she asks belligerently.

"I dunno. Curious."

She shoos me away. "Go be curious somewhere else."

"We're having a family party, and I don't feel like partying."

"Why? Is it your birthday and you're feeling your age?"

I give her bouncy ponytail a tug. "Enough with the wise-cracks about my age. You're only two years younger than me."

She holds up a finger. "*Younger* is the keyword."

We run in silence for a few moments. I'm feeling a lot better now that I'm moving.

She gives me a sideways look. "Okay, just tell me what's got your pants on fire that you're running hell-mell through Prospect Park."

"Hell-mell? Is that a word?"

"Spill it."

"My uncle just announced his retirement immediately—a huge fucking surprise to me, the one he handed over the company to. He's *gone*, off to Florida. Dad's leaving too. Everything's on my shoulders, all these jobs depending on me, and I've got big ideas with no clue how to make them happen, and it could all go belly-up on my watch after forty successful years in business!"

She stops running and stares at me. "That's the most words I've ever heard you say at one time."

I shove a hand through my hair. "Did you hear what I said? This entire business that's been going successfully for more than forty years suddenly dropped in my lap with no prep!"

She rolls her eyes and starts jogging again.

I can't believe this. I spill my guts, which I never do with anyone, and she rolls her eyes?

"That's it?" I bark. "You got nothin' to say to that?"

She holds up a palm, still jogging at a brisk pace. "You don't wanna hear what I gotta say."

I speak through my teeth, keeping up with her. "Yes, I do."

"Okay, you're being a drama queen. You've got a whole crew of brothers to help you figure this out. They're not going anywhere, are they?"

"No."

"Then take this for the opportunity it is, bring them in on everything, and make it more successful than it's ever been."

"That's your advice?"

She nods once. "That's my advice."

I think about this as we run. "That's actually good advice."

"See? I'm not just about stunning beauty." She winks, and I find myself smiling.

I like her. *Really* like her. And she's home for the first time in years. By herself as far as I can tell. "Your husband get you something nice for Christmas?"

She purses her pink lips. "Is that your way of asking if I'm single?"

"Yeah."

"I'm divorced, happy?"

"You okay?"

"It was mutual. Shoo now." She brushes a hand through the air. "Don't get any ideas about asking me to ride on the back of your Harley or get a drink or whatever you do with your women, because you could be the very last man standing in the apocalypse—I'm talkin' just down to you and me to keep the human race going—and I'd sooner eat you for dinner than hook up with you again."

I blink. What a bloodthirsty woman. To think I used to call her Airy Fairy for being such a girly girl. "You still mad at me for that one time?"

She stops running, so I stop too. She jabs a finger in my chest. "Do not *ever* bring that up again, you swine."

"You brought it up. Look, I was twenty. Can't you give me a pass for being young?"

"No."

"Why not?"

She lifts her chin. "Because I was also young, and *I* was not a swine."

"Is this because I didn't hold you after?"

She gestures wildly. "Why am I even talking to you? I came out here to get rid of my stress not add to it." She takes off at a fast run, and I keep up with her.

"Ariana, I'm sorry. I was a swine back then. In my defense—"

"Nope. No defense."

"I shouldn't have…whatever you think I did."

She halts abruptly. "I don't think. I know. You know too, but you're too much of a swine to admit it. Now go back to your family with your not-so-big problem while I figure out my life."

"What's to figure out?"

Her eyes narrow. "Go away."

"If I go back to my family, you're just going to be right next door. Then curiosity will make me have to stop by to see what your deal is."

"My dad would kill you."

"Ya know, I thought he was giving me the stink eye."

She parks a hand on her curvy hip. "Ever wonder what happened to the helmet you left behind in my bedroom?"

"I figured you trashed it."

"I did. I smashed the visor in and threw it in the garbage. Dad found it and recognized it was yours. Everyone knew you rode around on that Harley."

I lower my voice. "So he assumed I took his daughter's virginity?"

She stares at my chest. "Ma noticed the missing sheets. There was obvious evidence, and I didn't want to deal with it since I was leaving the next day, so I hid them in the bottom of a different garbage can." She lifts her gaze to mine. "They conferred on the sheets and helmet and confronted me. I confessed."

"You *confessed*?" I ask incredulously. "Why would you do that?"

Her chin juts out. "Because I was a good girl."

"You were." I can't help my grin at the memory of her back then, asking me to help her out while blushing like crazy. "You were also a dirty girl."

She looks away. "You ruined me."

My eyes widen. "What?"

She takes off at a run back down the trail, and I just stand there, staring after her fading pink. I ruined her? Is that why she never came home again?

My gut churns. I ruined innocent Airy Fairy? I feel horrible. She was this sweet little thing, and now she's a foulmouthed bloodthirsty woman. And it all traces back to me. I mean, I like her better this way, but maybe she would've turned out different if it weren't for me.

I slowly walk toward the entrance of the park.

Wait a minute. She can't lay all the blame at my feet. That was one afternoon. I mean, sure, I teased her when we were kids, but that's what kids do, right?

I wait outside the park's entrance. As soon as she heads for home, I'll join her and point out this obvious truth—if she's a foulmouthed bloodthirsty woman, it's not my fault.

Ariana

Ugh. Why did I say that? I push myself to run faster. Why not just tell him everything and complete the humiliation? *No one could compare. You haunted my erotic dreams long after you should've been gone. You always, always lingered in my mind. Hell no!*

I slow my run, my breath coming harder, and focus on one foot in front of the other, trying to get back to my usual Zen state while running. By the time I'm done the loop, I'm feeling more like myself.

I walk through the park entrance and yelp as a large man steps close. Then I see who it is and smack his shoulder. "Don't sneak up on me like that! I almost pepper sprayed you!"

Dylan stares at my empty hands. "With what?"

I fumble with the zipped pocket in my hoodie, feeling past my phone, a folded-up twenty-dollar bill, a crumpled tissue, and finally fish out the pepper spray, holding it up. "See?"

He rubs the back of his neck. "Gotta be a little quicker on the trigger."

I stuff it back in my pocket and zip it up. "Why're you stalking me? Don't you have a company to run?"

"Just answer one question, and I'll leave you alone."

I gesture for him to go on, though I really don't want to answer any questions. I'm so stressed right now I've started working out morning and night. Bad enough I'm recovering from a hard emotional hit. Throw in living with my parents for the first time since I was eighteen and it's stress city. I need to get a job and a place of my own quick. And Dylan is the very last person I'd ever confide in about any of this.

"How did I ruin you?" he asks softly.

Oh, hell. I never should've admitted it.

I head toward home, and he keeps up with me. "I don't want to talk about it."

"Ariana, I feel terrible thinking I ruined you somehow."

Warmth spreads through me at his sincere tone. Also, there's something really nice about the way he says my name. I let him off the hook.

"I shouldn't have said that. Obviously you didn't ruin me. I had a decent run in my marriage, a good job, yada, yada, yada. I'm just cranky, I guess. I'm not used to living at home again, and I've got a lot on my mind."

"Like what? Spill."

I clamp my mouth shut.

We pass Mr. McLaughlin, wearing his usual gray newsboy cap over his thin white hair. He gives us a nod. "Happy New Year to ya both."

"Happy New Year," Dylan and I say in near unison.

"Heard ya got a divorce," he says to me, his bushy eyebrows drawing down. "Musta been that California hippie's fault."

"Thanks, but it was mutual," I say evenly. Guess the whole neighborhood knows. *Thanks, Ma!*

Mr. McLaughlin shakes his head. "I told your parents not to let you go out to that Godforsaken place with all their yoga and New Age malarkey."

"On your way to Dooley's?" Dylan asks, reminding Mr. McLaughlin of his destination. "Say hey to Pete."

"Say hey yourself. Bye, you two. Get home before dark." He hustles off to his favorite bar, pretty spry for a guy in his eighties.

Dylan's lips curve up, his blue eyes twinkling. "He still thinks we're kids."

"I want kids," I blurt and slap a hand over my mouth. What is wrong with me? Maybe it's because I'm basically alone for the first time in years. I lost my friends in California in the divorce, and the ones I used to have here all moved to the burbs with families of their own.

We walk toward home in silence.

I glance up at him. He looks like he's thinking hard. I so wish I could take back my words. I've got baby on the brain.

"Why didn't you have kids with your husband?" he asks.

I suppose I'm a little desperate for a friendly ear, because I actually answer. "He didn't want kids. I agreed at first, and later I changed my mind." *And then we divorced, and now he's having a baby with Kiersten.* "I moved back to Brooklyn to be near my parents so they could be involved with helping me raise a baby."

He glances at my stomach. "You're pregnant?"

"No, soon, though. I have my sperm donor all picked out and, as soon as I get a job, I'm making the insemination appointment. Ma thinks that's nuts. She just doesn't get it." I take a deep breath, tense just thinking about my mother. She's on a campaign to get me married off fast before I move forward with the baby. At first it was just insistent nudges to call a friend's nephew or whatever, but this past week, she took matters into her own hands and surprised me (twice!) with a middle-aged single man sitting in the kitchen, waiting to meet me. She just doesn't understand I'm not ready for a relationship. It's only been two weeks since I found out my ex is going to be a father. They're so disgustingly happy I want to puke.

"Huh," Dylan finally says.

"Yeah," I say, glad he doesn't ask any more questions about my future child. I'm tired of defending my choice. Children are important to me, and I want what I've been denied before I miss my fertility window. "I need to get a job and a place of my own; then I'll move forward on the baby."

"What did you do out in California for a job?"

"Sales and marketing for a real estate development company."

"Huh."

He looks like he's thinking hard again. I don't volunteer any more information. I don't feel like thinking about my work with my ex and his family now. They've moved on to focus on the newest members of their family, and I need to move on too.

Finally, he says, "Maybe you could talk to my dad about that stuff. He's excited about getting his real estate license."

"And cross enemy lines? Ma would kill me."

He elbows me. "You let me cross enemy lines once."

I stop dead on the sidewalk and slam my hands on my hips. "Swear to God, Dylan, if you bring that up *one more time*, I'm seriously gonna kick your ass!"

He laughs. "You?"

I glare at him. "You're not doing much in the way of ingratiating yourself to me."

"Oh, *ingratiating*." He grins. "Is that what I'm supposed to be doing?"

"Yes."

He steps closer, his voice low and husky. "How's this? You're more beautiful, funny, and kickass now than you ever were way back when."

My lips part, my pulse racing. "So back then I was plain, boring, and meek?"

His gaze drops to my lips, my throat, and then back to my eyes. "You're missing the point. I'm complimenting you."

The air between us is suddenly charged.

I gulp. I can't go there. "You're trying to get in my pants again."

"Look, I know there's no defense for me for back then, but come on. Statutes of limitations are up, dontcha think?"

I focus on the fact that he is a pig. Not sexy. Not so gorgeous I can barely think straight when he's close like this, when I can see his thick lashes framing piercing blue eyes and the stubble I well remember scraping against me as he kissed me into a puddle of need.

My voice comes out hoarse. "I'm still the wronged party."

His head tilts to the side. "Did I invite myself up to your room, or did you beg me?"

"I so want to smack that smug look off your face."

He smirks some more. "Ya see. You weren't entirely innocent in all this."

"I was innocent until—"

"I helped you out with your little problem."

"We can stop talking now," I announce, heading for home at a brisk pace.

"Why did you pick me that day?" he asks.

I groan.

"You knew Sean better."

I wave that away. "Sean is like a brother to me. I've known him since kindergarten."

"So why me?"

"You are so one-track minded."

"I am when it's something interesting."

I stare straight ahead. "Fine. If you must know, it was because you seemed exciting. An older experienced man with a motorcycle."

"I guess two years older was a lot back then."

I let out a long sigh so he knows I'm not enjoying this awkward walk down memory lane.

"Why did you used to glare at me so much? I thought you were looking down your nose at me. You really surprised me, propositioning me that day."

I look to the sky. "I so wish this conversation was over."

"Just answer the question and I'll shut up about it."

I glare at him.

"Your glare back then was much more hateful."

I blow out a breath. "It wasn't hateful. I glared because you kept bringing up ballet, and I was forced to quit. It hurt to hear the reminder. 'Where's your tutu?' My answer was, buried like my dreams."

"Why'd ya give it up if it was your dream?"

I stop walking and lift my large breasts. "Because of these." I slap my hips and turn and slap my ass. "And this."

His smile is slow and sexy. "I like these and this."

I glare at him, and then I laugh. "Well, these and this don't go with a pro ballet career."

We continue toward home.

"Couldn't you just dance for fun?" he asks.

"It was tough to give up my dream. I couldn't feel the joy in dance after that."

Our houses come into view ahead, and we get quiet. Ma's probably watching through the window for me. She'll have plenty to say if she thinks I went for a run to meet up with one of the enemy. I can't even believe how long this feud has gone on between our families. Can we let the spoon thing go already? Maybe another guest took it home with them by mistake!

"Hey, you want to get dinner sometime?" he asks when we reach the sidewalk in front of our houses.

"Can't." I want nothing to do with a relationship, not for a very long time, and the last thing I want is another hookup with Dylan. I know he said dinner, but I also know there's chemistry, a *lot* of chemistry, and I know exactly where that would lead.

I glance toward the front window of my house, and the curtain drops. Yup. Mom police on the job.

He dips his head to catch my eye. "Just a drink, then."

"No."

"Too busy? Yeah, I get it. Unemployed, living at home."

My throat tightens, my eyes hot. "Screw you." I swore I would take time to heal after the shock of my ex moving on to the kind of family life he never wanted with me.

"Are you ever gonna forgive me?" he asks.

"It's not that," I choke out. "I'm just not ready. No dating, no relationships, no hookups, nothing."

He gets quiet.

I stare at the toes of his black sneakers. "Sorry."

He pinches my chin, lifting my gaze to his. "Don't be sorry, Ariana." There's a tenderness in his tone that nearly undoes me. I just haven't seen this side of him, and part of me wants to lean against his solid strength. I can't let myself be drawn in.

I force a neutral tone. "So, friends?"

He releases my chin and brushes my jaw with the backs of his fingers, making my skin tingle. "Yeah, friends."

I back away. "Great. Bye." I rush up the stairs to the front door and nearly stumble when I hear him get in the last word.

"For now."

5

Dylan

The next morning I'm over the shock of my uncle's retirement. Uncle Pat and I had a good talk last night at his retirement party, and he promised to show me his contact list and do a rundown of everything this week. On Friday we've got an appointment with a lawyer in the city to transfer ownership of the company over to me and my brothers. He leaves on Saturday. His RV is waiting for him in New Jersey, already packed. He sure did a good job of keeping his plans under wraps. I'm still not clear on why he sprang it on us this way. Maybe he just thought it would be a good surprise, like a gift, instead of the smack upside the head it was. For me, anyway.

I live close to our construction office in the Bay Ridge neighborhood of Brooklyn, so I walk the few blocks to clock in. My brothers and I, along with the crew, will drive out from here to a new apartment building in Queens. We're doing interior work, which I'm glad for because it's freezing outside again.

I've been thinking more on what the future could look like with me and my brothers owning a construction business and getting into real estate. Brooklyn is hot right now, and nearby boroughs could be soon. If we could get a piece of that action —buying up properties in run-down areas, renovating or knocking down and building new, and then selling high—that's some next-level shit there. And we're part of this community. I'd like to build parks and playgrounds into it, make it more than just a collection of apartments and commercial spaces. We'd be developing *neighborhoods*, giving back to our community. I need to do more research into it, but first I need the funds to invest.

No matter what my dad says, I don't feel right asking Gabriel for funds after he gave my dad that crown and scepter set worth a fortune. Then it hits me—my dad gave that to me. I bet it would sell for a lot at auction. Not just for the value of the piece itself but also the history of it. It couldn't hurt to ask my dad about hocking it. He does get in these moods sometimes, though, feeling nostalgic. He might want to keep it around just to admire it. Damn. I'd hate for him to regret letting go of it. I'm not sure what to do.

I open the door to our small first-floor office. It's two rooms and a bathroom. The front room has two desks for my dad and uncle, three filing cabinets, and a kitchen setup on a table in the corner. The back room is a meeting room with a long table and chairs. Nothing fancy, but it gets the job done.

My younger brother by six years, Connor, is leaning against my uncle's desk, waiting with coffee in hand. He's lean but strong and always neat, from his expensive haircut to his neatly trimmed beard. Sometimes I think out of all of us, he should've been the one to go to college instead of joining the family business. Don't get me wrong, he's good with his hands, but he's also thoughtful. Like maybe he's got a lot going on in that brain of his. He's the fourth in our band of brothers. My parents always say Connor was such an angel they decided to have another child, and then they got Brendan, who shocked them, being such a mischievous little devil. I'm pretty sure Garrett was an oops, because my dad got snipped after him, and that was the end of the line. Hey, six kids is plenty. It was fun growing up, but, looking back, I don't envy my mother trying to keep us all on the straight and narrow. She really tried.

"Morning, boss," Connor says. "Should I fetch your coffee?"

I jerk my chin at him. "Yeah, fetch me some bacon and eggs while you're at it."

He grins. "Leave it to Uncle Pat to make his retirement so dramatic."

I help myself to a cup of coffee from the pot he got started. "Right? Not a peep out of him, and then it's, by the way, the company is yours, good luck!"

The door opens and I glance over my shoulder to see Uncle Pat. "Just talking about your big announcement."

He smiles and stretches his arms over his head. "I'm a happy man."

"Better learn golf and bocce," Connor says. "You wanna fit in with the natives down there in Florida."

"Shuffleboard too," I say.

"I mostly wanna drive around on a golf cart." He pretends to be steering a cart. "Wouldn't that be the life?"

Connor and I exchange an amused look. Wouldn't be my go-to choice for fun but whatever.

"Dylan, have a seat at my desk," Uncle Pat says. "I'm giving you my computer so you'll have everything you'll need on it."

I glance at his ancient desktop computer, already thinking of how to get whatever info he's got in outdated software onto my laptop. I hope it's not too difficult.

"How 'bout at the end of the day?" I ask. "I gotta give the crew their task list for the day."

"Do it here and then delegate the supervision for a bit. I've got things to do, buddy boy."

"Yeah, all right."

After I assign the task list to the crew, I settle at his desk with him as everyone else files out. It's the longest two hours of my life. First, the computer takes forever to load up the files he wants to show me. And he talks so much before clicking the mouse I'm nearly catatonic. I show him how to do a screenshot so I can have it for later. By the time we finish, I've seen his accounting software, which my dad does and shares with him, and his contact directory, but I still don't feel like I know what I really need to know.

"How am I gonna keep bringing in new business?" I ask. "I don't have your network. I mean, besides this list of contacts."

He leans back in his chair, cupping his hands behind his head. "Yeah, people know me by reputation, so I get a lot of referrals. We'll put out a big announcement to my contacts about you as CEO once the transfer is official, and I'm sure people will go to you just as easily." At my skeptical look, he adds, "Don't worry! You'll get word-of-mouth going too, and soon you'll have your own network. It'll be fine. You gotta do some advance planning, though. Don't just think, oh, we've got a big job right now, so we're good, I'll stop looking for new work. *Always* be looking for the next couple of projects, yeah?"

"Yeah."

He claps me on the shoulder. "Good. I have every confidence in you. I've been getting you ready for this for the past couple of years. Why do you think I've been pulling you in on the business side so much?"

"Yeah, but I was never the one bringing in new projects. You had me step in once we had the project."

He inclines his head. "I like meeting people. Friends of friends become my friends."

"I shoulda been at those meetings."

"But I still needed you to manage crew. I couldn't pull you away too much or the projects would've fallen apart. You're ready, trust me."

Ready or not, here I go. "Thanks."

He stands. "Gotta run. Your aunt wants help packing up our apartment." They're putting their stuff in storage while they look for a place they like in Florida. They plan to live in the RV until they find the perfect place. He told us all about it last night at the *surprise, I'm retiring* party.

"One more thing," I say. "What do you think about adding a branch to the company? Rourke Management for future real estate development. Most of the value of the company is in the name Byrne Construction, so I want to keep that and add to it."

He grins. "I knew with your flipping-houses idea, you'd want to get into property development. I think it's great. Do what you want with the business as long as you keep it going." He wags his finger at me. "Just be careful not to get into deep debt. Start small and build from there. Build a cushion to cover payroll."

I straighten my spine. "Yup." It's all on my shoulders now, ensuring my brothers and our crew get paid. That's twenty people, all depending on me.

"See ya," he calls cheerfully, and then he's out the door.

I look around the empty office before focusing on his computer. I should email these files to myself, or put them on a flash drive. *Please tell me this thing doesn't take floppy discs.* I look around the back and find an input where a flash drive could go; then I dig around in his desk drawers for a flash drive and find nothing but mini Snickers, pens, pencils, and take-out menus. Fuck it. I'll just take the whole damn thing. I shut the computer down, unplug everything, and walk back to my apartment with it in my arms.

I set it on the dining room table and head downstairs to the basement garage for my Harley. I missed a ride to work on one of our trucks, so I have to find my own way.

By the time I get to the apartment building in Queens— newly constructed units in a reclaimed former piano factory —it's past eleven in the morning. I make the rounds, checking on the crew, and tell my brothers to take lunch with me at the diner down the block. The burgers are good there. Every one of them agrees no problem, except Brendan, the little devil, who is now what my mother calls "prickly" and I call "needs an attitude adjustment." He's twenty-five with a chip on his shoulder so big I'm surprised he doesn't walk crooked. The guy's got something to prove.

"Whatever you say, boss," Brendan says when I tell him to meet me for lunch. There's an edge to his voice I don't like.

I cross my arms. "That gonna be a problem for you? Me being the boss instead of Uncle Pat?"

He spreads his palms. "I'm an underling no matter what."

"You don't like working here, there's the door." I hitch a thumb toward the door.

His eyes narrow. "I'm co-owner now. You can't fire me."

"Who said anything about firing you? I'm giving you a choice—get on board or get lost."

He glares at the door like he's thinking it over.

"Why do you think Uncle Pat made me CEO?" I ask.

He turns back to me. "Because you're the oldest."

"Yeah, well, it's also because I've been working side by side with him since I could hold a hammer. I started working for him when I was sixteen, unlike the rest of ya, who coasted through high school and never had to look for a job because you had one waiting for you whenever you wanted it. I put in the time and the sweat."

"That was your choice to work construction in high school, and it was only part time anyway."

"So, what, you're gunning for my job?"

His chin juts out. "I want to be in charge of something."

"Like what?"

"I dunno. *Something.*" He blows out a breath. "I'm just restless."

I rub my jaw. "You play your cards right and I might have something for you."

His eyes widen. "Really?"

"Yeah, as long as you get on the Dylan-as-CEO train."

He laughs. "How many stops does it make?"

"Stops on your head if you don't watch yourself." I give his head a shove. "I'll see ya at lunch."

I wait until everyone's served up their lunch at the diner—we all got burgers—before springing my idea on them. I figure I've got a five-minute window to get it all out while their mouths are full.

"All right, I asked you guys here because I've got an idea for the future of our company." A rush of energy surges through me in anticipation of how big this could really be. "We branch out from just construction to real estate development. Properties are hot around here. Just look at DUMBO."

That was a run-down industrial area under the Manhattan bridge (Down Under the Manhattan Bridge Overpass) that was developed into an upscale mixed-use area of residential and commercial buildings. It's hip now and pricey, the most expensive neighborhood in Brooklyn.

"Properties?" Sean asks around a mouthful of burger. "Did Uncle Pat leave us a pot of money too?"

I shake my head. *I wish.* "We'd have to find the funds, but assuming I could get the money, what do you think? I want us to be neighborhood developers, adding parks and playgrounds, maybe a community center if we could swing it, as we build or renovate residential and commercial spaces. This could be really big for us, way beyond flipping houses. We'd be giving back while building neighborhoods."

All eyes are on me, burgers held in midair. I take them in —Sean, my go-to guy when I have to delegate; Jack, the quiet one always pulling pranks; Connor, the angel; Brendan, the devil; and Garrett, the beast (on account of his huge muscles). I've always looked out for my younger brothers, and now I'm officially in charge of them. I want us to be a team. They're smart and hardworking. I couldn't ask for a better crew.

"That sounds like a lot of work," Connor says. "Much more than we're staffed for." He goes back to his burger.

"We'd start small," I say. "Each project would help fund the next." Another surge of energy courses through me as I see how it could scale that way. "Dad could be our real estate sales guy, and he'd hear about property listings early too."

"That's probably why Dad's going in that direction," Sean says thoughtfully. "He knew about the retirement before we did. That's also why he was pushing us to ask Gabriel for funds."

"Yeah. I want to find another way, but what do ya think?"

"I'm in," Sean says.

My brothers grunt in agreement and go back to eating.

Sean pipes up again. "Do we know how to develop an entire neighborhood? We could go bankrupt with one mistake. It's risky. Not saying I'm not for it, just that we gotta know what we're doing before we take the leap."

I've been thinking about this ever since my talk with Ariana last night. I could pick her brain about her experience with a real estate development company. Even if she doesn't have all the answers, she could point us in the right direction. If she's really helpful, maybe I could hire her as a consultant.

"I know someone with experience in real estate development," I say. "Ariana Bianchi."

Brendan slaps a hand on the table, chews and swallows. "Consorting with the enemy. Does Mom know you intend to cross enemy lines?"

Sean gives me a knowing look. "He crossed them big time, from what I heard."

I narrow my eyes at him, the universal big-brother threat to *shut it* before I kick his ass.

"You and Ariana?" Connor asks, his glass of water stalling halfway to his mouth. "How did I miss that?"

"Neighborhood gossip," I say. "Anyway, she's back in town. I could ask her for some tips on what goes into development."

Sean taps the table. "None of this happens without the money. Where're we gonna get that kind of cash?"

I lower my voice, gesturing for them to lean in. "Remember that crown and scepter? It's gotta be worth a fortune. If Dad's okay with it, we could sell it at auction."

Sean scowls. "You can't sell that. It's Dad's royal thing."

"Which he willingly gave up," I point out.

"For the best woman in the world." Garrett, the sensitive soul hiding under bulky beastly muscle, says what we're all thinking. Dad always says that.

"It doesn't seem right," Connor says. "It's still an inheritance, passed down to him, and he passed it down to you."

"So is this company," I point out. "And maybe Dad would like the crown to help us instead of just sitting in a safe. I'll run it by him."

Everyone agrees if it's okay with him, we'll use it.

"I could be the guy scouting out new places," Brendan says. "That would be my domain."

"Sure, why not," I say. He wants a domain, he gets one.

He's as experienced as any of us at this new venture, which is to say not at all. "Once I do more research, you can all dig into a niche that will be your domain. Still need you on crew, though, for a while."

Everyone looks fine with it, so I finally dig into my burger. This could work with some startup cash. And it wouldn't just be picking up where Uncle Pat left off. It would be starting something new from the ground up, something my brothers and I can point to as our contribution to the Rourke family name. Like my cousins did in Villroy. This could be our kingdom in a way, except we're street royalty. I like the sound of that even better than sitting up in some palace living the soft life. This is where my family was meant to be all along. And I can't help but think with us being descended from royalty that we're about to launch a dynasty right here that'll keep going down the generations. I understand now why my dad cares so much about handing something valuable down to me, because now I could have something lasting to pass down to my own kids. We all can.

The Rourke dynasty starts now.

After work and a quick bite to eat, I head over to the Bianchis' place to see about a business dinner with Ariana for Friday night. By then, the business will be officially mine, and I'll know where I stand with Dad on turning the crown and scepter into something more valuable to me.

I find a spot to park on the street a few doors down. Ariana said no to a regular dinner, but a business dinner is no pressure. Truth is, I thought about her a lot after our run in the park last night. It's been a while since a woman really caught my interest. She's spirited, smart, and sexy as hell. Even with her fancy college degree and former California life-style, deep down she's just a girl from Brooklyn—strong and down to earth. I used to think she was uppity, glaring at me like she was better than me, when the whole time she was just hurt because my teasing reminded her of what she had to give up. If she would've told me at the time, I would've shut up about that stupid tutu. But she didn't, so that's that.

A voice in my head tells me to tread carefully with her. She's still reeling from her divorce. Thing is, I crave something real after years of shallow meaningless relationships. There were only two women I stayed with for a few months, but in the end, there wasn't enough there to keep us together. I can't help but think it's good that Ariana is eager to start a family. It means she wants to be settled just like me. When she's ready, maybe we'll take our friendship to the next level. Hopefully she won't already be pregnant with another guy's baby by then. Damn, things are already complicated.

And then there's the issue of our parents' feud. Okay, first of all, the feud was *not* our family's fault. It started with a neighborhood potluck at the Bianchis' house years and years ago. I was nine, I think. Our neighborhood goes way back to the nineteenth century with generations of Irish, Italians, Polish, and Germans who settled here back then and stayed, which is to say it's close-knit, people say hey to each other on the street, and they have potlucks. It's overwhelmingly Irish-American like my mother's family. The Bianchis are Italian, which means they go to the same church as us. Anyway, after the potluck at the Bianchis' house, Mom noticed that Dad brought her bowl back but no serving spoon. (Her hands were full with us kids.) So the next day she went next door and asked for the spoon back. Mrs. Bianchi claimed she never saw it.

Mom didn't call her a liar to her face—she's a classy lady —but she insisted it was there. Mrs. Bianchi insisted it wasn't, and Mom returned home furious, saying Mrs. Bianchi was a thief and a liar because she most certainly did see that serving spoon since Mom distinctly remembered her complimenting the pattern on the handle.

That spoon fight may have faded in time, but then right after that, the Bianchis got a mutt and never put up a decent fence around their postage-sized, mostly concrete backyard. The dog constantly got loose through a gap in their old wooden fence and preferred to take a crap in our grass backyard. Dad wanted to repair the fence, but Mom wouldn't hear of it. That was the Bianchis' responsibility.

Battle lines were drawn.

So Mom and Mrs. Bianchi refuse to speak to or acknowledge the other in any way, even though our houses adjoin and they go to the same church. Nothing gets by them, though. They watch each other and their families like hawks, always ready to pounce on any offense and tell their husbands, who are expected to dutifully relay the message to the other husband. The only reason I can think of for why the feud has gone on for so long is because Mom had too much time on her hands once me and my brothers got older. She volunteered at the school and the food bank, but still. Mrs. Bianchi gave her some real sharp focus when maybe she needed something to focus on.

I get off my bike and take my time on the short walk to the Bianchis' front door. I'm well aware I'm in enemy territory, starting with dealing with Mr. and Mrs. Bianchi, who've been giving me the stink eye for years. I'm prepared with my best manners and a peace offering. I was brought up right with manners, even if I don't always choose to use them.

I press the doorbell and keep my eyes straight ahead. If my mother is watching from next door, I don't want to catch the daggers of her glare. Or worse, her hollering over to find out what the hell I'm doing here.

Mrs. Bianchi answers the door. She's petite, fifty-something, with shoulder-length dark brown hair, no gray in it. Actually, her hair looks nearly identical to my mother's color and style, except Mrs. Bianchi has bangs. Do they go to the same salon? Wouldn't that be a riot, ignoring each other side by side in salon chairs while they got the same haircut? Her deep brown eyes shine through round brown-framed glasses.

She purses her lips, giving me the stink eye. "Dylan Rourke. Don't be sniffing around for my Ariana."

"Hello, Mrs. Bianchi. These are for you." I produce a bouquet of red roses from behind my back.

Her eyes widen. "Oh!" She giggles and puts a hand to her chest. "For me?" She grabs them and breathes them in. "I can't remember the last time I got roses!" She looks up at me. "Come in, come in. What're ya standing out in the cold for?"

First bridge crossed. I step inside to a layout nearly identical to my parents' house, except the Bianchis have the pocket doors separating the living room and kitchen/dining area closed. There's a couple of cushioned pale pink chairs and a faded floral sofa across from a TV mounted over a brick fireplace. Obviously Mr. Bianchi is grossly outnumbered in his house with a wife and two daughters. Flowers and pink to sit on. For his sake, I hope he has a man cave in the basement.

Mrs. Bianchi stares at me curiously, still clutching her roses.

I clear my throat. "Is Ariana around?"

"Yes, she's here." She holds up the roses. "I need to put these in a vase. Are you hungry? Follow me." She slides open a pocket door and heads to the kitchen in back. My parents reversed the setup with the dining room in back.

I follow her. "No, thanks. I'm not hungry, ma'am. I ate earlier."

She pulls a glass vase from a high cabinet and takes her time, filling it halfway with water and then arranging the roses. Finally she sets it on the center of the Formica-topped kitchen table, smiling at them, and then seems to remember me. "Sit. I've got some manicotti." She grabs a glass from the cabinet and fills it at the sink, saying over her shoulder, "You like manicotti?" She sets the glass on the table.

I really don't want to sit at the kitchen table eating when I'm not hungry. I want Ariana to show up here. "Actually, I just ate."

She crinkles her nose. "Your mother's cooking? No good. Let me get you a little something. Maybe some lemon cake." She opens the refrigerator door. Funny how she assumes I head home to eat. I've lived on my own for years.

"Could Ariana join us, ma'am?"

She takes out the cake and sets it on the counter, kicking the refrigerator door closed with a lifted foot behind her. "Dylan, I must say your manners are so nice to hear. Young men these days with their cussing and their—well! Never mind about those creepers!"

I can't help but poke the bear. "My mother raised me right."

"Hmph. Have a seat." She gestures to the red vinyl chair I still haven't taken.

I sit just so we can move things along here.

A few moments later, there's a slice of cake in front of me and a fork on a folded paper napkin. Mrs. Bianchi sits across from me at the rectangular table, looking at me expectantly. I'm not much for sweets, but I take a bite anyway. "Very good."

She leans forward, lowering her voice. "I want you to know that I know what happened between you two all those years ago, and I was *not* happy to hear it. To put it mildly."

Your daughter asked me to! But I can't throw Ariana under the bus—she already confessed to the crime and probably heard all about her parents' displeasure on the long drive in a U-Haul truck out to California for college—so I take a big bite of cake and say, "Really good lemon cake."

"It's done." She brushes her hands together like she's wiping away that dirty business. "She's moved on. You're both single and of marrying age, so you have my blessing to continue on as you were."

I nearly choke on the cake stuffed in my mouth and grab my drink, tossing it back with watery eyes.

"As long as it's not in my house," she adds.

Thank you?

I set my water down. "Good to know. I, uh, appreciate it, ma'am." Who knew how far a bouquet of roses could take me? All the way into Ariana's bed with her mother's blessing.

Mrs. Bianchi studies me intently. *Will I ever get to see Ariana?* I think Mrs. Bianchi wants to lay out the terms before she calls her daughter from wherever she's hiding.

She folds her hands on the table in front of her. "You have a good job, I hear, CEO of Byrne Construction."

"Did Ariana tell you that?" Because it's not common knowledge yet. Uncle Pat wants to wait until it's official before announcing the change in ownership. If Ariana was talking about me, that's a good sign.

She waves a hand airily. "Just word on the street."

It occurs to me where she could've heard it. "Did my mom tell you about me being CEO?" They haven't spoken in years as far as I know, but I can't think of who else Mrs. Bianchi would've heard it from. My dad wouldn't cross enemy lines, and my brothers know to keep it quiet until Uncle Pat announces it.

She huffs. "We're not on speaking terms. I told her we're not speaking to each other, and she agreed. She just announced it when she happened to be bringing in the garbage cans at the same time as I was getting the newspaper. It wasn't a *conversation*. Just word on the street."

Oh-kay. Guess it's important to keep each other informed on how great their kids are doing. Some kind of weird one-upmanship going on there.

She gestures for me to eat more cake I don't have room for.

"Is Ariana upstairs?" I ask.

She lifts a finger and hollers to the ceiling, "ARIANA! Your gentleman caller is here!"

I stifle a laugh. Haven't heard that one before.

She smiles serenely. "She'll be down in a minute." She watches me, so I take another miniscule bite of cake.

Ariana appears a few moments later, her brow furrowed until she sees me, and then she relaxes. "Oh, it's you."

"Expecting another gentleman caller?" I ask with a grin. She looks cute in a turquoise and black striped sweater with faded jeans and owl slipper socks. Her dark brown hair is down, sexily tousled, and long enough to wrap around my fist. No makeup. She doesn't need it. She's a natural beauty.

"You don't even want to know," she says, looking meaningfully toward her mother.

"Ariana!" her mother exclaims cheerfully. "Dylan brought me a gorgeous bouquet of red roses like a proper gentleman caller. Show some gratitude. It's not every day you find a man who knows how to court a girl properly."

Court a girl? Mrs. Bianchi is more old-fashioned than I realized. She must've went through the roof when Ariana confessed about hooking up with me. *In her childhood bedroom.* I got off easy with the stink eye. And it seems I lucked out with my timing coming over here because Mr. Bianchi isn't home from work yet. I don't think the roses would've had the same effect on him. I'm not sure what would've helped with him other than humble gratitude for allowing me to talk to his daughter.

"Ma, we're just friends," Ariana says firmly.

"That can change," her mother carols.

Ariana looks to the ceiling before landing her big brown eyes on me. "Thank you for getting my mother roses," she drones dutifully. Then sounding more like herself, she asks, "What's up?"

"I wanted to see if you were available for a business dinner on Friday."

"Business dinner," she echoes. "We have business to discuss?"

"Yeah."

"She is!" her mother exclaims. "She's got *nothing* on her calendar whatsoever! I've been telling her, put yourself out there. Sign up for one of those swiping dating apps, swipe up, swipe down, just do something! Or go to the church bingo. I mean, sure, the bingo people are a little older, but they have grandsons. All you hafta do is ask."

I grin at Ariana, who looks like she's torn between rolling her eyes and screaming. Apparently, Mrs. Bianchi is in a hurry to get her daughter back in the dating game.

Her mother stands and heads for the lemon cake on the counter. "Here, sit, Ariana. Have some cake with your handsome man friend."

Ariana holds up a palm. "No, thanks. And, Ma, please, the divorce just came through. Would you stop with the get-a-man routine?"

Her mother abandons the cake to cross to my side and elbow me, saying in a stage whisper, "This one. Divorce came through six months ago, and they were separated for a month before that." She turns to Ariana. "You think your eggs are getting any younger? Uh-uh. These are the same eggs you were born with. Thirty-one-year-old eggs do expire. You want a baby so much, and I'm happy for that eventuality, believe you me, but you need the man first. A *husband* man not an *anonymous picture* man in a binder. That kind of man could be a lunatic."

Binder?

"Ma, I told you it's all digital now; there are no *binders of men*." Ariana throws her hands up. "And who do you think is on those dating apps? Anonymous picture men."

"But then you get to know them, unlike"—her mother lowers her voice like it's unspeakable—"*those binders.*"

Ariana parks a hand on her hip. "Maybe I should just swipe right on a baby daddy app."

Baby daddy app? Oh, right. They must be arguing over the sperm bank thing.

Her mother bristles. "Don't get fresh, Ariana Madalene! There are no baby daddy apps. Thank gawd!"

"Madalene," I mouth at Ariana.

"Shut up," she mouths back.

I stand. "So are you available on Friday?"

"She's available," her mother answers for her.

Ariana sighs. "Yes. Dinner on Friday for *business*."

"And maybe some pleasure too," her mother throws in.

I can't help my laugh. I have an ally.

Ariana flushes pink. "Ma!"

Her mother lifts her palms. "What? You hafta speak plainly. You don't have time to beat around the bush with your expiring eggs."

"Great," I say, fighting a laugh. "I'll pick you up at six."

"Sure," she says flatly. I'm not sure if her lack of enthusiasm is because of me, or her mother embarrassing the shit out of her.

"Wait! Are you picking her up on your motorcycle?" her mother asks in a horrified tone. "No, no. You can take my Honda. Much safer. Oh, Dylan, you didn't finish your lemon cake. Hold on. I'll just wrap it up for you to take to your bachelor pad." She takes the plate and carols over her shoulder, "Must get lonely over there."

I ignore that, even though, yeah, it's gotten stale living alone. "Thanks, Mrs. Bianchi." I wait while she gets my to-go cake ready. Ariana looks tense, so I wink at her.

She shakes her head.

Her mother hands me the cake wrapped in aluminum foil with a smile. "There you go."

I tuck it into the pocket of my leather jacket. "Thank you, ma'am." Then the devil gets the best of me. "I'll tell my mother you said hello."

She scowls. "We're not on speaking terms."

No-o-o. They just occasionally brag about their children in broad general announcements when they're in hearing range of each other.

"You should be," I say. "You have a lot in common, both being beautiful vibrant women." Yeah, I'm laying it on thick, but this *whatever it is* with Ariana will go easier if our mothers aren't at war.

Her mother giggles. "Oh, stop! You flatterer you." She smooths her hair, smiling.

I turn to Ariana. "See you soon."

I head out just as her mother says loudly, "Don't blame the child for the sins of the mother, I always say. Walk the man to the door!"

"We're just friends," Ariana says. "He can find his way out."

"That's not the way he's looking at you. Shoo. See him to the door."

I stop and turn, halfway into the living room. Mrs. Bianchi gives me a big thumbs-up and a wide smile, and then gives Ariana a little shove in my direction.

Ariana makes a face and crosses to my side. "Allow me to walk you the six feet to the door."

"Seems like the right thing to do for your gentleman caller."

She lowers her voice. "I can't even...please do *not* encourage her."

"What's she talking about, a man in a binder? Is that about the sperm bank?"

"Never mind. She shares too much."

"Too bad our mothers aren't on speaking terms, because they could talk all about how we're both single and have never given them grandchildren." And my mother has thankfully never been so in-your-face as your mother, I add silently. Though she drops hints.

"No comment."

I grin. Her mom is a riot. It's funny when it's happening to someone else.

"What's this business dinner about?" she asks when we reach the door.

"I wanted to pick your brain on real estate development. Something I'm thinking of getting into with the construction company."

Her brows shoot up. "You have the funds for that?"

"I'm working on that part. In the meantime, you and me, dinner." I step closer, and her lips part. "I'm looking forward to it."

Her eyes search my face. "I hope you don't think—"

"No pressure. Just business." *For now.*

She glances toward the kitchen and back to me. "My mother goes too far. I just don't want you to get the wrong idea."

"I like your mom."

She lowers her voice and leans so close I breathe in the delicious scent of vanilla. "I like her too, but she drives me crazy."

I want to taste her, touch her soft-looking skin, but restrain myself, pulling away. "Good night."

"Night, Dylan," she says softly.

I head out into the night, a smile on my face and lemon cake in my pocket. Mission accomplished.

6
———

Ariana

Is this weird? Yes, it is. I'm going to dinner with Dylan Rourke, the swine I planned to avoid for the rest of my life. I change for the third time into a soft, pale gray cowl-neck sweater, jeans, and black ankle boots. I check myself out in the full-length mirror, brushing some lint off my jeans.

"This is not a date," I remind myself as my stomach does a slow flip.

I don't even know where we're going to dinner. I don't have his number to ask about dress code, and I'm not calling his construction office to ask. So how do you dress for a business dinner with a guy who typically wears leather and denim?

I turn away from the mirror. This is good enough. I'm getting way too worked up for a business dinner.

Dylan and I have never had a date. We've had one afternoon fuck and years of a battle he was unaware we were having. I should've told him to shut up about the ballet thing when we were kids instead of feeling hurt and angry. How was he supposed to know he was hitting a nerve? I was such a shy good girl back then I couldn't get the words out. Now I'm so used to working with people I seem to have lost my shyness. It comes up now and again, like if I suddenly find myself at a party where I don't know anyone, but for the most part I'm comfortable in my own skin.

I head downstairs, where my parents are suspiciously loitering in the living room when they'd normally be eating dinner. Dad's an electrician and always comes home before six on Fridays for pizza night, which they make together from scratch. Tonight they're pretending to watch a home-decorating show, but really they want to see if my "gentleman caller" comes to the door. Dylan will earn major points if he comes inside to greet them versus pulling up to the curb and beeping his horn or texting for me to come out. Ask me how I know this. My parents are lying in wait to see if he passes the test. I have *got* to get a place of my own.

"Is that what you're wearing?" my mother asks, eying my jeans. "Come upstairs. I have a cute skirt that should fit." Which would be great if I wanted to dress like my mother at Sunday church.

I hold up a palm. "I'm good, Ma, thanks."

"She looks fine," my father says.

My mother glares at him. "She has to look better than fine, Tony! How many men of marrying age are knocking on our door?"

"One?" my father says with a straight face.

My mother nods. "That's right, one. And Ariana wants a baby, and I want her to have a husband first."

"So we like Dylan now?" my father asks me.

"We're friends," I say.

"He knows what's what, I tell ya," my mother says. "Good manners, shows respect for his elders and, despite whatever his mother is guilty of, he cannot be blamed."

Thank goodness Dylan has never falsely accused my mother of stealing a serving spoon! He'd never be allowed to go near me. Considering how shocked my parents were about the whole virginity incident, they came around to Dylan pretty quick. Guess he's preferable to an anonymous binder man. Or maybe any man they know from the neighborhood would do. The bar is set low when it comes to getting me safely married before producing their much-wanted grandchild. It doesn't seem to matter to them that I'm still reeling from the shock of my ex starting a family without me so soon after our divorce. I know I'm not ready to risk my heart for any man.

The unmistakable roar of a Harley pulling up has us all looking toward the front window.

My mother leaps from her chair, clasping her hands together. "He's here! Quick, Ariana, go change. I'll stall him."

"I'll get the door," my father says, rising from his chair and tucking his light blue T-shirt into his belted jeans. "We need to have a talk, man to man."

I stifle a groan. You'd think I was sixteen again. "Dad, please, that's not necessary."

He smooths his thinning dark brown hair over his bald spot. "It definitely is."

My mother calls to me from the back of the house. She moved fast. "Ariana, if you're not changing, could you help me with something in the kitchen?"

I hang my head. She's trying to get me out of the way so Dad can have his man-to-man talk with Dylan. This is so embarrassing. Although, it'll be even more embarrassing to actually witness the man-to-man talk, so I take the easier route of escape. "Coming, Ma."

I make my way back to the kitchen, where my mother is pulling the pizza dough from the refrigerator. "Why must he have a man-to-man talk with Dylan?"

My mother tsks. "Your father had the same talk with Mark, and now look, he married Rosalie and they have three beautiful daughters." That's my sister, and I sincerely doubt Mark needed to be talked into committing. He was crazy about Rosalie from the day they met.

She hands me her car key fob. "You can let Dylan drive if you like, I don't mind. I'd just feel better if you weren't on the back of the death machine."

"I'm sure he's a good rider. He's been riding motorcycles since he was seventeen."

"Not with my daughter on the back." She plants her hands on her hips and gives me a thorough inspection from hair to toes. "Are you sure you don't want to consider a skirt now that you know you won't be on the wheels of doom?"

"I'm sure. It's really not a date. He wants to ask me about my work."

"Sure, sure." She gestures for me to go back to the living room. "Get out there now. Too much time with your dad and he's likely to invite him to stay for dinner. Me, I understand young couples need time alone to let things percolate."

I bite back a sharp remark. She's just not getting it that I'm not looking for a man. I know she loves me. It's just a tad overwhelming at times. "I'll see ya later."

"You stay out as late as you like." She gestures broadly. "Overnight is fine if you need more time to get to know each other. We won't wait up."

I cannot believe she's giving me her blessing to hook up with Dylan on our first nondate. This is the same woman who gave me a lecture about a man not buying the cow when he could get the milk for free. "It's a business dinner, Ma."

She kisses my cheek. "Good luck with your business, sweetie!"

I stifle a groan. "Thanks."

I return to the living room to find my father and Dylan standing in the center of the room. Dylan's head is tilted to the side, listening to my father speak in a low conspiratorial tone.

"Okay, I'm ready." I hold up the key fob to the Honda and jiggle it. "And I've got our ride."

Dylan straightens and gives me a slow sexy smile that actually makes me blush. Heat creeps up my neck and down my chest. He's dressed casually, but nicer than usual in a chambray button-down shirt with dark jeans and nice leather shoes. His thick dark brown hair is on the longish side, combed back and still damp from a shower. He's got light scruff on his square jaw.

Not a date, I remind myself. Business.

My father slaps Dylan on the back. "Good to see ya again, Dylan."

"Likewise, Mr. Bianchi," Dylan says.

He gestures for me to go ahead of him, and we head out the door. He's wearing cologne, a spicy masculine scent that makes me want to lean close and breathe him in. Dammit. This is not good. I can't risk getting involved, especially when I've got plans for becoming a mom on my own very soon. What man would want to step into that scenario? Me, pregnant with another man's baby. I will *not* be acting on this inconvenient lust. I will *not* be thinking of how good it was that one time. That was likely due to the newness of everything for me, chemistry, and my low expectations. Yes. Chemistry and virginal low expectations. Stick to the plan. First step, finding a new place to live before my parents drive me insane. I've only been home for three weeks, and I'm not sure how much longer I can take the harassment over finding a man.

I wait until we're on the sidewalk before saying, "Please ignore whatever my father said about me. He's overprotective."

One corner of his mouth quirks up. "He wanted to be sure I know that you're special. Not someone to treat lightly and run out on."

I groan. "That's his subtle way of letting you know that he knows what went down back in the day."

He looks up and down the street, probably checking for nosy neighbors. "So you told your parents all the grisly details?"

"Well, I was trying to prevent a war between our families. I said you were a chickenshit who bolted right after we did it, and I hoped to never see you again."

He blows out a breath. "Yeah. That was a dick move. I've matured since then, and I'm glad you're willing to see me again."

"That was *almost* an apology."

He takes both my hands in his, enveloping mine in his warm firm grip. His blue eyes are direct. "I'm sorry."

I believe him. "It's okay. I forgive you."

"Good."

"Our ride's just down the way," I say, heading a few doors

down to my mother's black Honda Accord. I hand him the key. "I'll let you drive the chariot."

He opens the passenger-side door for me and waits for me to get in before shutting it. Wow. I had no idea he had such nice manners. I bite back a snarky comment about his badass rep being ruined as he gets in the driver's side. But really it's an unusual thing in guys. Maybe there's more to him than I realized.

He takes me to a restaurant in Cobble Hill that's cozy with a full bar and a row of tables for two and four across from it. White light bulbs strung along the top of the bar and rows of white candles on each table glow warmly against the dark cherry wood tables, dark wainscoting, and dark glossy hardwood floors. I'd go so far as to say it feels intimate, romantic even.

And we're here for a business dinner, which is all I want or need at this point in my life.

He orders a local Brooklyn IPA, and I get myself sparkling orange wine just because it sounds fun.

When the drinks arrive, he lifts his bottle toward me. I lift my glass, and we clink bottle to glass.

"Cheers," he says at the same time as I say, "Salute."

His blue eyes sparkle as he tips the longneck bottle up to his mouth. My gaze drops to his throat as he swallows. Why is that sexy? He's just so much man—wide shoulders, strong corded neck, chest chiseled with muscle that stretches the fabric of his shirt. My ex was more of a tall, thin, neat desk-job guy. Okay, he was squeaky clean with a neat hair part and clean shaven. The near opposite of a rugged man who works with his hands. My gaze drops to where Dylan's shirt is unbuttoned at the top, revealing tanned solid chest. My pulse kicks harder.

I lift my gaze to his, and he gives me a knowing look. Busted! I take a sip of my sparkling orange wine and promptly choke. My cheeks burn as I cough my way right back to awkward-teen-on-a-date territory.

"You okay there?" he asks.

I nod, my eyes watering. Finally, when I can breathe

normally again, I take a sip of water and set it down. "So what kind of questions did you have for me?"

"I'll ask you after we order. How are you?"

"Me? I'm, um, fine."

"Bored?"

Extremely. "I keep myself busy on the job hunt."

"Anything good come up?"

"No. Maybe I'm being too picky. I want something cool that makes me jazzed to wake up in the morning and get to work."

"It's a job not a theme park."

"I know. I guess with my fresh start I was looking for something to grab me." I squeak in surprise as he lunges across the table and grabs me by the upper arms.

He laughs and releases me.

I shake my head, my heart racing. I'm not used to someone so physical, and he startled me. "Well, that woke me up. So, how are you?"

"Great. Just signed the papers this morning, and Byrne Construction is all mine. And my brothers'. We also added a branch for real estate development, Rourke Management. Why not just go for it, right? Even though we're still construction right now, I want it to encompass more." His eyes gleam. "I want to build an empire."

I actually get chills. That is the kind of excitement I want to feel for my career. "That's awesome."

He grins. "Thanks."

The waiter stops by for our order—shoulder steak for him, roast chicken for me—and Dylan gets down to business.

"Tell me everything you know about running a real estate development company."

"Err, that could take a while. I worked in sales and marketing. My husband, my *ex*-husband, scouted out properties. It was a family-run business, so there were often meetings where I heard what was going on in all departments. I wasn't heavily involved with the construction branch."

"I got that part covered. Keep going."

So I do, starting with finding the properties, to developing them, working with the local community to make sure it would be a good fit and there wouldn't be any holdups from local stakeholders. It was mostly commercial properties with the occasional apartment building. My job was primarily to find tenants for the buildings.

Our food arrives, and Dylan lifts a palm. "Enjoy your meal. I'll ask you more questions when you're done eating."

"Oh. It's no problem to talk and eat."

"After is soon enough," he says and cuts into his steak.

This could be a very long night. I'm not used to such a slow pace, but I find I don't mind it so much. He has a quiet strength that actually makes me relax. I focus on my food. Everything is delicious, from the juicy chicken to the crispy thin potato slices and baby spinach.

"This is really good," I tell him.

"You appreciate good food like me," he says. "Do you cook?"

"I know the basics. I just never got into cooking, I guess. It always feels like a chore."

"I cook."

I can't hide my surprise. "You do?"

"Yeah. Self-taught. It's relaxing for me."

"What do you make?"

"All sorts of things. Risotto, lasagna, enchiladas, chicken cordon bleu. I just try stuff out and, if I like it, I keep the recipe." He takes a sip of beer, his gaze direct. "Maybe one day you'll get to try my cooking."

I swallow hard, shifting my gaze toward the bar. He's interested in more with me. I need to stay strong and protect my heart, no matter how he surprises me with his manners or his physicality or his cooking. Did I ever really know him?

I turn back, watching him cut another piece of steak, and try to see him with new eyes as the man he is now, not the evil torturer of my youth or the callous young man who bolted on me. He's gorgeous as ever with those chiseled features and muscular body, but also a man who knows what he wants. A good man, I think. He's been really nice to me, and he even apologized sincerely for his blunder way back when.

"Want a taste of my steak?" he asks, offering me a forkful.

"Sure." He surprises me by feeding it to me, our eyes locking with an intensity that brings a flush of heat straight through me. After I finish the bite of steak, I keep my eyes on my plate. "Very good. Did you want some of mine?"

"No, thanks."

We eat in silence for a few minutes. I steal a glance at him, and he looks content to just sit and eat. I'm actually surprisingly relaxed besides the occasional hot flash. Normally I'm a ball of tension on a first date. I can't help but feel that's what this is. Just the two of us in an intimate restaurant sharing food and conversation.

"Is this a date?" I ask.

His fork freezes in midair. "It's whatever you want it to be."

"What do you want it to be?"

He sets his fork down. "You want me to spell it out?"

I grip my napkin in my lap. "That would be nice."

He leans forward. "I like you. And it's not about your looks, though you are beautiful and sexy. I like the other stuff even more."

My breath catches. "What other stuff?"

He grins. "You're a foulmouthed bloodthirsty woman. I appreciate that kind of spirit. It's real and honest."

I'm taken aback. "I am *not* a foulmouthed bloodthirsty woman."

He arches a brow. "You said you'd eat me in the apocalypse."

My jaw drops. "And that made you like me?"

"I appreciate a strong woman. I want a partner, someone to share the good and bad and make the load just a little lighter."

I gulp. "You sound like you're looking for a wife."

"Not exactly. I'm just tired of meaningless hookups. I'm looking for something real."

"Oh, I'm not."

His lips curve to the side. "No, you're just sperm shopping."

"Shh! Eat your dinner." I go back to eating and give him a pointed look.

He smiles and takes a bite of steak. Odd. Most guys would be a little freaked that the woman they took out to dinner is looking to start a family soon.

We finish the meal in silence, but I can feel him studying me. He wants something more from me, and I'm not ready for that. I'm recovering from a hard emotional hit. My ex wanted babies but not with me. He's living the life I longed for *with her*. The bastard.

Dylan's deep voice cuts through my dark thoughts. "Why would you be ready for a kid but not the family to go with it? Don't you know how important a father can be to a kid? My own dad taught me and my brothers so much. Boys need their dads. And girls too. My mom says her dad showed her by example what made a real man, which was why she knew instantly when she met my dad that she finally met her match. You love your dad, don't you?"

I hadn't thought of it in those terms. "Yeah, I do. A lot." My dad is a solid, steady presence in my life. He's always the voice of reason when I'm lost, and I always knew he loved me.

"There you go."

I study him for a long moment. He's the oldest of six brothers, which means he has experience with young kids, and I always saw him looking out for them. He's good-looking, strong, and healthy. I think he's pretty smart too. Not just by the way he talks. Once in school they gave our class an IQ test, and his brother Sean scored the highest. I bet all the Rourkes have those smart genes. They didn't choose to go to college, preferring to work a different kind of job in the family business. He's an ideal specimen.

My heart races at the thought I don't dare say out loud. Could I get the father part without the husband part? He could be my sperm donor, but still be involved in the child's life. Is that too crazy?

Yes. That is crazy.

Maybe just a donation quietly done at the sperm bank? At least I can confirm he's not a lunatic for those concerned about such things. *Mom.*

I'd have to offer him something in exchange. Maybe one donation for free business consulting whenever he needed it? I'd have to come up with some definite terms, some kind of ironclad contract.

"You're giving me a really strange look," he says.

I wave that away, my mind still cranking on possible ways we could both benefit from an arrangement. "Sorry, just tired."

"It's only a little past seven."

I force myself to focus on the conversation. "I've been getting up at the crack of dawn to work out." This is actually true. I need the quiet time to myself and the workout to get rid of stress.

"Yeah? I do that too."

The waiter arrives with the dessert menu. I order the lemon bar, and Dylan gets the carrot cake.

"I'm not much for desserts, but the carrot cake here is the best I've ever had," he says.

"I'm partial to lemon. That's why we had lemon cake at home. I made it, actually. I like baking better than cooking."

He smiles warmly, and I find myself smiling back. "Yeah? It was really good. Tell me more about how the real estate development company worked."

Determined to show my value as a future business consultant, I tell him all about the company I used to work for. One of the cool things they did was to incorporate art into the area they developed, a sculpture or mural on a building usually. They wanted to give back to the community.

His eyes light up at that last part. "I really like that idea of building community when you build. I had a similar idea, but instead of art, building a park with a playground, where the kids can run around a bit. I know that was something my brothers and I loved when we were kids. Looking back, I don't know how my mom did it, having the six of us high-energy boys tearing through the house all the time."

My ovaries do a happy dance. Dylan gets it. The dad thing. The kid thing. I can't help but look at him now and think baby daddy. I know it's crazy. But what guy has ever taken me out and talked to me like this about family and fatherhood? Maybe he's trying to give me a hint that he wants that too. Or maybe I just have baby on the brain.

Chill, Ariana! Job first, place to live, then baby.

Our desserts arrive. I bite into my lemon bar, and it's too sour. I break off some of the crumb topping to eat instead, and then I just watch Dylan enjoy his carrot cake.

After a few moments, he notices me watching him and not eating. "You don't like your dessert?"

"It's okay."

He slides his dessert over to me. "I'll share."

I take a bite and it's effing delicious. He's extremely polite with the dessert, unlike my ex, who would take, take, take while I savored and usually wound up with only a few tiny bites. Dylan takes a bite and waits for me to take one before taking another. It gets down to one morsel of scrumptious cake left, which is really his turn, and he sets his fork down.

"You can have it," he says.

I take the last delicious bite, my belly happy, my ovaries dancing, and my heart full. "You're actually a wonderful man."

He grins and indicates the empty dessert plate. "All it took was carrot cake to get back into your good graces."

"You could be my baby daddy," I blurt.

He doesn't flinch, merely studies me for a long moment.

I hold my breath, part of me hopeful and part of me appalled for even suggesting it. We barely know each other as adults. It's just not how it's done. I can't even get the words out to explain what he'd get in return.

I can't believe I said that!

He leans forward, his blue eyes gleaming in what almost looks like triumph. Did he want this all along? "I have some conditions."

7

Dylan

Rourke family philosophy—be bold, take risks, you only get one life. I'm living it right now. Big changes coming with the business and now personally. Deep down, Ariana and I want the same thing—to settle down and have a family. I've known her my whole life. She's good people.

Is it the best time for me to start a family? Not the best, but not the worst either. I mean, sure, I need funds to get into real estate, but the construction side of the business is solid. And Ariana would be an asset to our real estate business. Plus, I've got five brothers invested in a positive outcome since we're all co-owners. And I own a three-bedroom co-op. I think that's a solid enough foundation. There'll never be a *perfect* time. Life happens, and you roll with it.

She's looking at me strangely again. Somewhere between wary and happy. I'm offering to give her the baby she wants so much that she got a divorce over not getting to have one. What an idiot that guy was. Ariana would be a great mom, strong but kind, and I've always seen myself as a father down the line. Suddenly it's right here, right now, and I'm good with it, as long as the two of us are solid.

First, I lay out my terms. "Here's what ya hafta do. Drop your perfect sperm donor guy at the sperm bank. Take your name off the list or whatever ya need to do. You're gonna hold off on that until we see how things are working out with us."

"Us?" she asks, her voice high and reedy.

I know she's not ready for a relationship. But the last thing I want is to be a sperm donor. I want the real deal with a real family. She's just gun-shy after her divorce. That was six months ago, which seems long enough for her to date again. I should be more freaked about this. I mean, I was angling for dinner or a drink. The start of something. But this is where she's at, and it doesn't scare me one bit. I'm thirty-three years old, CEO of my own business, a homeowner. I'm ready for a family.

"You hate living at home," I say. "All that pressure to get a man, right? Move in with me and that all goes away."

"For how long?"

My jaw goes slack. Of all the things I thought might come out of her mouth—thank you! Really? Are you sure?—that wasn't one of them. First time I ever offer to live with a woman and she's already looking for an out. I witnessed the insanity of her home life. I've got a three bedroom, plenty of room. Not that I'm offering to be roommates, unless she needs time to get used to the idea of sharing my bed. I won't mention the extra bedrooms; see how it plays out.

"What do you mean for how long?" I return, letting my irritation show.

She leans forward, her voice soft. "Dylan, I know you don't love me and I don't love you. This would just be, you know, so we get to experience parenthood. Of course, you could be part of the baby's life. I know you'd make a great dad."

"Thanks." My mind searches for the right solution. There's definitely chemistry between us. Seduction isn't even necessary the way she's so eager for my sperm. Ha! When has that ever come up before? It occurs to me that maybe there's more to the end of her marriage than she let on. Divorce can get nasty. I've seen it with friends' divorces.

I keep my voice low. "Your divorce came through six months ago, so why didn't you move back home then?"

Her expression closes, her hands dropping to her lap. "I told you it was amicable. I had a good job at his family's company, and everything was fine."

"You need to be honest with me if we're going to do this family thing together. What sent you running back home?"

"I didn't run," she says tightly. "I made a conscious decision that it was time to move on with my life."

I push her because I want her to be real with me. "And you move on by being unemployed and letting Mommy and Daddy take care of you?"

"Go to hell," she snaps, her eyes flashing. "You have no idea what it's like to go through what I went through."

"You married young. Now you're not."

"Thirty-one is still young."

"Not with your stale eggs."

She glares at me.

"He robbed you of your youth and denied you what you wanted most. What else? What sent you running home? Did he parade around his hot new girlfriend? More than one?"

"I didn't run! I made a conscious decision that it was time to move on."

I signal for the check. "Yeah, okay."

She gets quiet, worrying her lower lip like she's considering whether or not to tell me the truth about what went down.

I pay for the meal, and a few minutes later we're back in the car. She's still quiet. I keep quiet too, hoping she'll confide in me. This isn't going to work if she doesn't trust me enough to tell me stuff.

I start the car, and she puts her hand on my arm. "Yeah?" *Come on, come on, be real with me.*

Her voice comes out hoarse. "My ex paraded around his hot new girlfriend, and she was eight months pregnant. He was thrilled to be a dad, and they plan to marry soon."

"Are you fucking kidding me?" I bark. "He's happy to be a dad with her but not..." I clamp my mouth shut. Hell, that's gotta hurt. And he got this other woman pregnant before their divorce. What an asshole. No wonder she's so wary.

"Not with me. Exactly." She wipes her weepy eyes. "What's wrong with me?" Her voice cracks, and my chest aches in sympathy.

I wrap an arm around her shoulders and pull her in close. "Nothing's wrong with you. That guy is a fucking idiot who doesn't know a good thing when he's got it."

She leans her head against my chest. "I don't know why you're being so nice to me."

"I'm a nice guy."

She laughs a little and looks up at me. "Somehow I missed that about you."

I pinch her chin. "Look, I'm ready to settle down, and you'll do just fine."

She blinks a few times. I can see I've surprised her with my bold declaration. Not often a guy offers commitment on a first date.

"Wow," she finally says.

"Yeah." I take my arm off her, put the car in gear, and pull away from the curb. "You're the first woman in a really long time to snag my interest."

"Wow," she says again.

I laugh. "Okay, I'll take a double wow."

She clears her throat. "Yeah. So I really appreciate it, ya know, but forget what I said earlier. The truth is, you deserve to have someone in your life who can, um, *really* appreciate what you have to offer."

The fact that she says it like that tells me she thinks I've got something worth offering. It's just a matter of time, getting her comfortable with me. It's like at work when we got that big job at the old brewery and basically built a new building from the ground up. It looked like an overwhelming task to get it all done on time and on budget. So what did we do? We scoped out the parameters of the project and worked backward, breaking it down into steps. Small goals, short deadlines. Checking things off the task list until it started to take shape before our eyes. It's all about breaking down the big goal into small steps. Baby steps for Ariana. I smile to myself at the baby reference. Baby goal takes baby steps.

"Your family always did have a flare for the dramatic," she says with a smile, shaking her head. Like she wasn't the one to bring up wanting my sperm. I don't mention that fact, though, because I suspect she still wants it and just needs to warm up to the idea of us. I'm not trying to rush into marriage and baby, but I need us to happen before she gets herself pregnant with some lunatic's baby. Yeah, I'm taking Mrs. Bianchi's side on this one.

"Whatta ya mean flare for the dramatic?" I ask in mock offense. "The feud? Cuz that was not *our* fault."

"Well, my mother certainly had no reason to steal a serving spoon. We've got two full sets of silverware, one for everyday and one for holidays. No, I'm talking about the whole royal thing. So dramatic. I'm sure that was just a rumor you guys spread to get with girls."

"That's actually true."

She scoffs. "Right."

"My dad would've been king if he hadn't abdicated the throne. I'm the crown prince, which means I was next in line to be king after him."

"Be serious. Your dad works construction."

"You got some time? I could show you proof at the office."

"Sure, why not. Show me your proof. And it'd better not be some lame-o Halloween costume of Prince Charming."

I pull out into traffic. "Like I'd ever pass for Prince Charming."

"Right?"

"You didn't hafta agree so fast." I grin. "The office isn't far, down in Bay Ridge."

"I'm in no hurry to get home. I'm sure my parents are doing their usual date-night thing."

"Which is?"

She sighs. "They make pizza together, watch an old movie from their dating days while they cuddle on the sofa, and then they go upstairs to finish what they started."

"From your tone I'm guessing it's not the movie they're

finishing."

"Yup. I've learned to stay downstairs and put the TV on high volume. Not that they're all that loud, but you know bedsprings. Sometimes the headboard hits the wall, and there is the occasional—" she coughs "—noise."

"I can top that."

"You can?"

"Oh, yeah, one time I let myself into my parents' house with my key—this was after I'd moved out, so I was probably twenty-one—and there they were, naked in the living room. First thing I see is his ass. He's got her bent over the sofa and they were going at it *hard*. I tell ya, there are some things you can never unsee."

"Ugh! Dylan! Did you have to give so many details? Now I can picture it. I don't think I'll ever look at your parents the same way again."

"I wanted to puke. The closed living-room drapes should've given me a clue, but I just never expected anything like that."

"Did they see you catch them?"

"Yeah. Mom said, 'Dylan!' and then Dad turned and pointed toward the door. He had no plans to stop. Not embarrassed in the least either. I was intruding, and he wanted me gone. Not like I wanted to stay and watch. I was just frozen in shock. I left so fast I nearly killed myself stumbling down the stoop. And I've never gone back in using my key. I always ring the bell and wait however long it takes for them to put themselves back together."

She giggles. "They must've been married more than twenty years by then. Good for them."

"Yeah, good for them, bad for my burned retinas."

"You knew they must've had sex at least six times to have you guys."

"I didn't want to think about it, let alone see it."

"Understandable."

I relax. Things are back on track between us. Conversation is easy, and we can laugh together.

"So what's your proof that you're royalty?" she asks. "Are

ya hiding a throne in your construction office? Ya know, that's what my dad calls a toilet."

"You'll see. I don't wanna spoil the surprise." I stop at a red light, pull out my phone, and click over to my pictures, handing it to her. "Here's a bit of proof. I just went to my cousin's wedding on Villroy Island. That's my kingdom and that's the palace."

She shakes her head. "This pic is from a distance just like any tourist could get."

I chuckle and shove my phone back in my pocket. "Don't pretend you're not into the royal thing. I distinctly remember you approached me to help you lose your V-card because you heard I was a prince."

"That was just a pickup line, and you said it wasn't true."

"That was a pickup line?"

"Yeah. You were supposed to say 'Yeah, I am.' Then I was gonna say 'I always wanted to be with a prince.'"

I glance at the light and hit the accelerator. "You had it all worked out, didn't you?"

"I did. I planned it for weeks."

"With me?"

"I narrowed it down to you."

"Who else was in the running?"

She waves a hand in the air. "No one worth thinking of for more than a few minutes."

"Sean?"

"I told ya he's like a brother to me. I can't think of the boy who ate a booger in first grade as a potential lover."

I laugh. "How long was I in your sights?"

"I don't know. A week? Two?"

"So you've had a thing for me for a long time now. I think the royal thing will cinch the deal now that I know you secretly wanted to be with a prince." I slap the steering wheel. "Damn, I shoulda been using that angle all these years. Why did I keep it close to my chest?"

She laughs. "Seriously, though, if you're really a royal, then how come you're not rich?"

"Because my dad was exiled for marrying a commoner.

He started with nothing here in Brooklyn. Have you ever noticed his accent? He doesn't sound like us."

"I don't think I've ever heard him say more than good morning to me. Occasionally, I'd hear him barking orders to you or your brothers when you were outside."

"Yup. In a commanding tone because he's used to people running to do his bidding. And believe me, we listened."

"Now that I think about it, he does sound a little formal in his English."

"Yeah, it's from his upbringing on Villroy, though he tries to hide it and throw some slang in there."

She stares at me. "I'm actually starting to believe you."

"Good." I pull into the lot behind our office, park, and turn to her. "Prepare to kiss my feet."

She laughs, shaking her head. "Never gonna happen, Rourke."

"That's Crown Prince Dylan Rourke to you. Or you could just call me your highness."

"Ha!"

I walk with her around the building to the front entrance, where I do the security code to shut down the alarm system.

Once inside, I flip on the lights. "Proof is in the safe." I head for the back storage closet and shift some jackets out of the way to reveal a large safe in the wall. Uncle Pat used to offer a discount if a customer paid in cash, so that's why he got the safe. My dad put an end to that practice because it meant it wasn't on the books, and that was not exactly cool with the taxman.

I do the combination and pull out the box. I turn to find Ariana sitting on the edge of a desk, her legs crossed, one leg swinging. She straightens as I approach, uncrossing her legs, her eyes wide.

I set the box on the desk next to her and undo the metal latches. "You go ahead and lift the lid."

She leaps off the desk and stands in front of the box. "I swear if a bunch of fake snakes spring out of this box, I'm gonna throttle you."

"There's that bloodthirsty side I like so much."

"You're crazy."

"Open it."

She slowly lifts the lid as she cringes, peeking at it with one eye closed. She relaxes and stares. "Oh my God, you are a prince! Can I touch it?"

"You can touch anything of mine," I say in a husky voice.

She's too enthralled to take the bait. She carefully lifts the crown out and admires it from all sides. "It's breathtaking!"

"I was thinking of selling the set at auction to get some cash for buying up properties." I ran it by my dad, and he said he needed time to think about it, though he could see my point in getting something for it. Seems like a strong possibility I'll be able to use it.

"Oh, Dylan, you can't! This set is gorgeous. It belongs in a museum." She carefully sets the crown back in the box and pulls out the scepter, tracing the cross at the top with a look of pure wonder on her face. It is a magnificent set, but what good does it do me sitting in a safe in the back of a storage closet?

"It belongs to me," I say. "I can do what I want with it."

She tears her eyes away from the scepter and stares at me. "It belongs to the royal family. You're supposed to pass down heirlooms like this."

I lift one shoulder. "The line stopped with my dad. He abdicated the throne, and that ended our portion of the event."

"You said this is yours. He passed this heirloom down to you."

"Only cuz he felt guilty that I never got to live the royal lifestyle."

She sets the scepter back in the box and turns to me. "You're supposed to give it to your firstborn."

"Maybe it'll be our firstborn. You on board with us?"

She swallows visibly and runs a shaky hand through her hair. She's scared. She wants the baby part without the man in her life, but that's not gonna work for me. Besides, I'm pretty sure she'll come around to the idea of us.

"I'm not gonna marry you right away," I tell her to put her

mind at ease. "We'll test the waters a bit first. You move in with me."

"Oh, God. This is crazy."

"Which part?"

She throws her hands up. "All of it!"

I tip her chin up, and my eye catches on a vein in her neck pulsing rapidly. "So you only want me as your baby daddy, nothing else?" I lean down and kiss that throbbing pulse point, my hand sliding under her long hair, cupping the back of her neck as I kiss along the side of her neck. Her skin heats, her scent so sweet; I nuzzle in more, breathing her in.

"Dylan," she says in a breathy voice, "do you actually want to marry me? You didn't sound like you were all that excited. You said I'll do just fine, not exactly romantic or…" She trails off as I rub the scruff of my jaw against her neck before biting her earlobe and giving it a tug. Her hands grip the front of my shirt. Baby step in the right direction—she's touching me back.

I lift my head to meet her eyes with a grin. "Wouldn't be the worst thing that ever happened to me."

"Gee, what a charming proposal."

I wrap her long hair around my fist like I've wanted to since I first saw it. "We could be good together, Ariana, if you just gave us a chance. I wanted dinner or a drink. You want my baby. You tell me what's the best way forward."

"Let's keep it simple. You make a donation at the sperm bank. I'll be your consultant for free whenever you need me."

"That's not simple. That's fake. I want something real."

She stares at my mouth, and I know what she wants. What we both want.

"I'll grow on ya," I say before my lips meet hers.

Her lips are soft and yielding, exactly right. I deepen the kiss, tasting her, and an electrifying jolt of lust shoots straight through me. Her arms wrap around my neck, and she's fully on board with the kiss. It's hot, it's urgent, it's fucking amazing. Her hands roam over my back and down to my ass, pulling me close. *Fuck, yes.* I knew it would be like this. She wants me, and I am rock hard.

I break the kiss when she moans deep in her throat. "You'll move in with me."

Her breath comes faster, her eyes searching my expression. She pulls away, and I let her go, giving her a moment.

Her fingertips rest on her lips as she stares at me, and I hold her gaze.

She turns and starts pacing. Still thinking.

I grab the box with the crown and scepter and head back to the safe, putting it away. I turn back to find her standing completely still, her eyes closed.

"Ariana," I say before pulling her into my arms.

Her hands go to my waist, holding me lightly. She licks her lips and stares at my chest. "I just got out of a marriage. Ya think I want to jump into another relationship so soon?"

"I told ya I want something real."

She stares at my neck. Getting closer to eye contact. "Can I think it over for a few days?"

"Sure, if you come back to my place right now."

Her eyes snap to mine, narrowing suspiciously. "For what?"

I give her a slow sexy smile. "So we can get to know each other better. I'm telling ya, I'm gonna grow on ya."

She smiles. "Like a fungus."

I grab her by the shoulders, and she squeaks. "That's right. All over ya." I run my hands quick-like over her face, shoulders, and arms, careful to skip the erogenous zones.

"Sure, what the hell," she says.

"Now that's an enthusiastic yes if I've ever heard one." I'm being sarcastic.

"It's better than trying not to hear my parents go at it."

I take her hand and walk out with her. "Just what a guy wants to hear. Spending time with me is better than listening to your parents fucking nearby."

She laughs.

I stop just outside the door to do the security code.

"I can't believe you're really offering to give me a baby," she says from behind me.

I turn. "I can't believe you wouldn't date me but you want my baby."

"It just seems simpler. A transaction of sorts. I was actually thinking of offering my business consulting for your sperm at dinner before I dismissed it as insane baby fever." She pauses. "I still blurted out the baby thing, though. I don't know why I keep blurting stuff out to you."

"Because I'm awesome and you sense that deep down."

She doesn't even laugh; instead she just looks thoughtful as I walk with her to the back parking lot to the car. I unlock it, open her door for her, and shut it behind her.

When I get in the driver's side, she asks, "Have you ever lived with a woman before?"

"No." I start the car and pull out into the street. It's a short drive to my place.

"Have you ever had a serious relationship?"

"A few."

"How many is a few?"

"Two."

"That's a couple."

"Oh, okay. Guess that's important to be real clear like that. A couple of relationships. Didn't work out."

"How long were you together?"

"Why does it matter?"

"Because I need to know if you're good at relationships."

"Doesn't that kinda depend on the people involved?"

"No. A relationship requires good communication and trust. I'm good at that. Are you?"

I set her mind at ease. "Look, you can talk as much as you like. I'll listen. And I'll never cheat on you. I don't see the point in making a commitment if you don't intend to honor it."

"Well, that's good to know, but that's not what I meant. I mean, you know, intimacy, opening up to each other and really getting to know the other person inside out."

I bite back the dirty thoughts that come to mind. But I sure would like to know her inside out. I go with a neutral comment. "I'm up for anything."

"What if you can't get me pregnant?"

"Then I will die trying." I grin.

"I'm serious! What happens then?"

"We could adopt. The point is to have a child, right?"

"Yes," she says softly.

"We're not having a baby right away, though. A stable loving home is important. To start, we're just gonna get to know each other. Intimately."

She lets out an audible breath. "Oh." A beat passes before she says, "What do you mean by intimately?"

"Same thing as you did."

"Sharing of confidences?"

"Sure. Among other things."

I pull into the underground garage and park in my space. She's out the door before I can open it for her. I lock the car, take her hand, and walk her to the elevator.

"I'm nervous," she says.

I give her hand a squeeze. "Don't be. It's like riding a bike. You had a crash, but you'll remember everything the moment you ride again."

The elevator doors open, and we head inside. I punch the button for the eighth floor.

She gives me a strange look, her brows drawn together. "I can't tell if you're talking dirty or just talking."

I shake my head. "Believe me, you'll know when I'm talking dirty. Relax, we're just gonna do the intimacy thing you wanted."

"Ya see, even that sounds suggestive when you say it."

"Then you say it."

She licks her lips. "We're going to become intimate and really get to know each other inside out. Gah! It sounds suggestive when I say it too!"

"That's what I like about you, Ariana. You say what you mean, and you mean what you say." I give her a quick kiss.

She's speechless. Sex appeal, I got it, and I know how to use it.

The baby thing is a maybe. Ariana is a maybe. Still, I can't help but think we're heading in the right direction.

8

____

Ariana

My heartbeat roars in my ears and my stomach drops as the elevator ascends to the eighth floor. Am I about to have sex on my first date with him? More alarming, are we really going to get married and have a baby together in the near future? Did we just decide that on our first date?

My breath is shallow, and I'm *this close* to hitting the button to go back to the lobby. And then my breath leaves my body when Dylan suddenly shifts, backing me up against the wall. He boxes me in, his hands on either side of my shoulders, his face millimeters from mine, those blue eyes up close burning with such intensity I can't even blink.

"Relax. You're safe with me," he says before brushing a kiss so light across my lips that I grab the front of his shirt to ensure I get more.

He brushes a light kiss again, and I sigh, my eyes closing in surrender. He presses another kiss to the corner of my mouth and then the other corner. I follow him, seeking more. His big calloused hand slides up my throat, his thumb trailing to the sensitive spot just under my jaw, his fingers curling around the side of my neck.

I wait, breathless, my pulse skittering, every nerve ending at attention. Finally, he kisses me in a deep drugging kiss that's exactly what I need. My mind clouds, all panicky thoughts vanishing. Desire pools low in my belly, my limbs heavy as he presses close, his leg wedging between mine, his hard body pinning me against the wall. I'm throbbing and achy and all I can think is *more.*

He breaks the kiss, his thumb brushing just under my jaw. "Your pulse is racing, Ariana."

"I know."

"Scared or excited?"

"Both?"

He smirks. "You don't know? I'll have to do better than that."

The elevator dings for the eighth floor, and he pulls away, taking my hand, and guiding me out to the hallway. My legs are shaky. I can't believe I'm so worked up over going back to his place. I mean, obviously if I want his sperm, I have to get close to him. He already said he's not cool with dropping off a donation. And it's not like we haven't had sex before. Just not with high stakes involved. Last time I knew I was leaving the next day. This time I may be tied to him forever.

"Your mom would approve of me over a lunatic, dontcha think?" he asks.

I burst out laughing. "I don't know why she's stuck on lunatics being in binders of men at a sperm bank. It must've been some weird story a friend told her."

He stops short before leaning down and kissing my neck in the sensitive spot just under my jaw. "You're calming down. All I have to do is make you laugh."

"Was that kiss to check my pulse?"

He winks. "Among other things." He grins and places a hand on the small of my back, walking me to his place. After he unlocks the door, he gestures for me to go in first.

I step into the kitchen and stare in shock. I was expecting bachelor pad—spare with a bench press and barbells or something. It's actually really nice, like I could totally see myself living here. The kitchen is modern with stainless steel appliances and a light tan granite-topped island. On the other side of the island is a dining room with a light-toned wood table that seats eight and herringbone hardwood floors. There's even a nice buffet cabinet with a round honey wood mirror mounted above it. Exposed brick along the windows on the adjacent wall look original to the building. This Harley-riding construction worker has classy taste. Of course, he is a prince. I'm still trying to wrap my mind around that one.

"You like?" he asks.

I turn to him. "Yes, it's so nice! Did you decorate it yourself?"

"Yeah, pretty much. Just picked up stuff here and there."

"I was expecting bachelor pad."

"You gotta understand, I see a lot of interior design working on residential buildings. You get a feel for it. I like clean lines and natural materials."

"Me too."

He smiles, his blue eyes sparkling. "Good." He takes my hand and pulls me to the adjacent living room, which looks comfortable with a light brown sofa with a chaise lounge on one side of it. A wall-mounted TV with a storage cabinet under it are directly across from the sofa. He even has plants. What bachelor takes care of plants?

I stare at him as he goes to the window and pulls down the venetian blinds. He's responsible. He's a nurturer of his younger brothers and plants. His father appeal just shot up exponentially! There are *four* different kinds of plants. I have no idea what they're called, but they're green and thriving. And it's neat! There's no stuff anywhere. Just a couple of remotes on an end table next to a lamp.

He opens the cabinet under the TV, and a few moments later, music plays. It's mellow, low-key. I don't recognize the band. I bet it's his seduction playlist.

He turns to me. "There's also three bedrooms, but I didn't want you to think I was putting the moves on you, giving you the tour of them. C'mere, Airy Fairy."

"Don't call me that."

He holds his palm out to me. "Ariana, come here." There's an edge of authority to his voice that I respond to instinctively, dropping my purse and crossing to him.

I place my hand in his, and he surprises me, lifting my hand over my head and twirling me around. He twirls me back and pulls me in close.

"How's that feel?" he asks.

"Nice."

"I remember you best twirling around, a look of pure joy on your face. You should dance again. Go ahead." He steps back and watches me.

My cheeks heat. "We could just, you know, slow dance together."

"Give it a try. Just a little of that ballet you loved so much you couldn't ever stop dancing."

I blow out a breath. "I can't. It's been too long, and I feel weird with you watching."

He closes the distance, placing one warm hand on the small of my back, the other hand taking mine. "Okay, then, we'll dance together."

I rest my hand on his shoulder, a little unnerved because this all feels so much more romantic than I'd ever antici-pated from him. He draws me in even closer, the warmth and spicy masculine scent of him surrounding me. I rest my cheek against his chest, listening to the solid thump of his heart. We're dancing, barely, just a slight sway as he holds me.

A few moments later, the tension drains from me. The easy rhythm he sets, the soft music, the heat and strength of him— it's exactly what I need. And it's been so long since I've been held.

His voice rumbles in his chest. "Maybe you could dance when you're alone and get some of that Airy Fairy lightness back."

I lift my head. "I always hated that nickname."

He strokes my hair, his gaze tender. "Is that how I ruined you? By teasing you too much, and then taking you up on your offer?"

I press my lips together. I hate to admit the truth but, at the same time, it clearly still bothers him that I said that.

He brushes his thumb across my lower lip, leaving a tingle

that makes my lips part. "You want me to kiss you again, Ariana?" His voice is velvet, and everything in me melts.

"Yes."

I go up on tiptoe, but he keeps his lips frustratingly out of reach. Instead his hand slides down my spine in a slow heated trail before settling on the curve of my ass. My breath catches, the heat of his hand burning through my jeans, my entire body heating in response.

His eyes lock on mine as his hand slides lower, cupping me, his fingers pressing firmly between my legs. I suck in air. I hadn't expected the intimacy of the touch, yet I don't pull away. It feels too good. He caresses me, sliding back and forth. My hands grip his powerful shoulders, my knees weak. I'm liquid heat, melting from the inside out, a heavy ache building inside me.

His eyes smolder into mine as he continues to stroke me intimately. "Tell me how I ruined you, and I'll give you what you need."

I have no doubt he knows exactly what I need.

"You're not playing fair," I say, even as my hips shift restlessly up against him, seeking more contact.

"No, I'm not." He holds me by the hips, stilling me. "Tell me."

I huff. "No one could compare, okay? You ruined me for other men was the rest of that embarrassing sentence."

He stares at me.

I babble on because I'm in this far, and I'm a sparking ball of need. It's been so long, and he's so good at making me feel good. "Every guy was a disappointment. Not one guy took his time with me the way you did, not until I met my husband, which is probably why I married young. I didn't think I'd ever find it again."

His lips curve up for a moment before he frowns. "Now why would you say it like that? Ruined you."

"I don't know. I just blurted it out. You caught me off guard that night, and I was already on edge from my mother wringing her hands over my future." I tense just thinking about my mother. "Kiss me again quick."

He cups the back of my neck, drawing me close, and nips my lower lip, sending an electric jolt of lust straight through me. "I take my time with everything, you know. Work and play. I want to do it right, not fast."

I grab his ass and pull him against me. "I love that."

He cups my jaw, his thumb stroking my cheek. "You didn't ruin me for other women."

I deflate and drop my arms from him. "Lovely. Just what I want to hear."

He frames my face with both hands. "But I never forgot you."

I stop breathing. "Oh."

His hands drop to my shoulders, trailing down my arms to my hands, which he holds in a warm firm grip. "It was hard to know you were married, and I'd never have the chance to be with you again to see what might have been. Yet here you are."

"Here I am."

He smiles against my lips. "You want me to ruin you again?"

I throw my arms around his neck. "Yes. I ache for you."

He mutters a curse before his mouth slams over mine. His kiss is hot and demanding, and the world falls away as need grows within me. His fingers spear through my hair, his other hand cupping my ass, holding me tight against him. I only want to get closer. I want to merge with him. I yank his shirt out of his jeans, sliding my hands up his broad back, needing to feel skin on skin. The hard play of muscle only makes me want to feel more of him, see more, taste more.

He breaks the kiss and wraps my hair around his fist, giving it a tug and exposing my neck. I'm nearly vibrating in anticipation before he dips his head, his lips meeting my throat gently before he opens his mouth, his teeth scraping against me. I shiver. There's something about the way he handles my body that I never forgot. It's confident and commanding, consuming me, but with a restrained power that lets me know he's being careful with me in the best possible way. Cherishing me.

"Ready for some of that intimacy?" he asks in a strained voice.

"God, yes."

He takes my hand and leads me to the sofa. Strange. I thought we'd be heading to one of his three bedrooms. A three bedroom is awesome for a family.

He takes a seat, and I take a seat on top of him, straddling his lap. He immediately lifts me by the waist and sets me on the sofa next to him.

I sit there, completely confused. What just happened?

"Tell me everything about you," he orders.

"What happened to ruining me?"

"Priorities. Focus, Ariana. Hurry up and tell me everything."

I glance at his jeans, which are straining tight across a massive erection. He's checking things off the list I said I wanted—get to know each other first. Why did I say that? I just want him to get me off. Can I say that without sounding like I'm desperate and horny? Hell, I am desperate and horny. Probably doesn't help that I haven't been with a man since my ex more than seven months ago.

His tone is of utter calm and patience. "I'm sensing you're not fully on board with the intimacy thing. This was *your* idea."

I take his hand and place it on my upper thigh. "First thing you should know about me is I haven't been with a man in more than seven months." I spread my legs and stare straight ahead, hoping he'll take the hint.

"It's been three months for me," he says, spreading his legs just like me.

I'm torn between a laugh and a scream of frustration. Obviously, he's trying to share intimacies, mirroring me, and that should be worthy of praise. On the other hand…I shift his hand to my inner thigh. "Could you just—"

"What?"

"I'm throbbing."

His brows lift. "And?"

My cheeks heat. "And could you, um, please help me out?"

"Could I help you out?" he echoes like he's confused.

Yes! Get me off!

I'm just desperate enough to explain further. "Yeah, you know—ah!" I'm flat on my back because he just tackled me.

He holds himself up over me, grinning. "Horny, dirty girl."

His lips meet mine as he fits himself between my legs, the hardness through his jeans rubbing exactly where I need him. A moan escapes as my nails dig into his shoulders, my hips lifting for more. He makes no move to strip, me or him; instead he kisses me hungrily, his hand sliding down to cup my breast, caressing it through my shirt, and then finally under my shirt, his fingers slipping under my bra to pinch my hard nipple. He grinds against me, and I see stars. And then there's nothing but his mouth devouring mine, his hips grinding against me, my insides coiling tight and hot. I'm so close.

He lifts his hips off mine, and I'm about to protest when he quickly undoes the button and zipper of my jeans, yanks them down, pulls my boots off, jeans go next, and finally returns to me, his hand sliding inside my panties. I groan loudly at the intimate touch I craved.

"So fucking wet," he says, his fingers thrusting inside me. I gasp, and then I'm panting as he thrusts in and out. Need coils tight and hot. He shifts, the heel of his hand applying just the right pressure in a slow rub as his fingers stroke me on the inside. I'm suddenly right there, teetering on the sharp edge of release.

"Please, please," I whimper, need overwhelming me.

He presses his lips to my neck. Hot, open-mouthed kisses trail up to my ear as his fingers work me expertly in a steadily increasing rhythm. I moan softly, my toes curling up as my body tightens around his fingers.

"Let go," he orders, and then his teeth sink into my neck in a sharp bite.

My body jerks and I explode, white-hot pleasure rushing

through me, sparking all the way down to my toes. He gentles his touch, murmuring praise as I ride out the most delicious orgasm of my life. I collapse into the sofa, limp.

His hand slips away, and he kisses my jaw, my cheek, my lips. "Beautiful."

"I needed that so badly," I announce.

"I think I'm getting the hang of sharing intimacies with you."

I grab his head and kiss his smiling mouth. He scoops me up and carries me to his bedroom. I rest my hand on his bicep, hard with muscle, in a dreamy haze. He sets me on my feet next to his bed and pulls my cowl-neck sweater over my head.

He hisses out a breath as he takes me in. "Sexy," he says before his mouth meets mine. His hands slide from my hips up my sides to my breasts. My fingers fumble on the buttons of his shirt. I need to feel him skin on skin against me. He breaks the kiss, brushes my hands away, and unbuttons his shirt, his heated gaze never leaving mine.

I go for his jeans, unbuttoning and unzipping over his thick erection. Then I drop to my knees and kiss him through his boxer briefs. He groans. I peel off his jeans and briefs and he helps me, kicking off his shoes and stripping. Finally I've got him right where I want him, and I wrap my hand around him in a firm grip, stroking up and down. His fingers grip my hair tightly. I lick my lips and take him fully into my mouth. He groans again. I keep going, loving the taste of him, loving hearing his pleasure. I watch as his head tips back, his eyes closing.

A few minutes later, he gives my hair a sharp tug. "Ariana."

I look up at him, and his eyes burn into mine. "Yeah?"

He lets out a strangled groan before yanking me to my feet, his mouth crashing over mine. Within seconds my bra is off, panties too, and he tosses his shirt to the side before pushing me back on the mattress.

"Not getting you pregnant until you're mine," he says as he grabs a condom from the nightstand.

A spark of pure joy lights up within me over his openness to a baby, even though he sensibly wants to wait. He wants a family and, deep down, as scared as I am to risk my heart, I'd like that too. I'm sure when the orgasm wears off, I'll find the idea of our committed future alarming, but right now I'm exactly where I want to be.

His voice is gravelly. "Spread your legs, baby."

I open my legs and he groans, taking me in. He covers me a moment later, the sensation of skin on skin bringing a sigh of relief and then a gasp as he thrusts fully into me. He lifts his head, watching me as he slowly pulls nearly all the way out and thrusts hard. We both groan.

"More," I say, lifting my hips.

He grips my hip tightly with one hand as he thrusts, the intensity climbing as he increases the rhythm. His breath is harsh by my ear. "You feel so fucking good."

I shiver. "You too."

He pulls out suddenly, shifting to kneel between my legs, and sets my ankle over his shoulder, pausing to kiss my calf before setting my other ankle over his other shoulder. He grips my hips firmly and thrusts, the deep penetration stealing my breath.

"Oh, God," I gasp out, and then there are no words as he thrusts deep over and over. Intense pleasure spreads throughout my body as he hits just the right spot. My eyes roll back in my head, my fingers fisting in the sheets.

"Look at me."

I focus on him with great effort. His large muscular body above me, the power and strength of him as he thrusts deep again, I've never felt anything like it. An incredible ache and pressure with an escalating intensity that makes me want to get even closer. I can't move though, caught in his grip. Close. So close.

He pumps deep again and again, and the pressure builds with each thrust. It's too much. *I need, I need.* I can't form the words. My breath comes in short pants. Our bodies are covered in a sheen of sweat. His eyes burn into mine, the tendons of his neck pulled tight with his restraint as he slides his fingers between my legs and strokes me. My head arches back, a soft keening sound escaping as my entire body tenses under him.

His voice, deep and hoarse, urges me on as he pounds into me, his fingers stroking faster and faster. "Open your eyes, Ariana. You feel how I own your body right now?"

I force my eyes open. "Y-yes."

He gentles his touch, and I tremble. He thrusts deep and stills, his fingers stroking me lightly. "You like it."

It's not a question. I'm fever hot, trembling, achy, and barely hanging onto a thought. His fingers still, and I nearly howl. "Dylan." I mean it as a protest, but it sounds like a moan.

"You want to come now?"

"Yes."

"Watch what I do to you."

I look down, seeing where we come together as his thick cock pumps deep, his fingers stroking me expertly. A low sound begins in the back of my throat as I shake with need.

Drops of sweat form on his forehead, and I see what it's costing him to keep control.

"Give it to me," I half-beg.

He stills again, buried deep, and his hand slides up to cup my breast, his thumb grazing back and forth over the tight peak. I slide my hand down to touch myself, desperate for release, and he grabs my wrist. "Only I touch you."

I meet his eyes burning into mine, and a whimper escapes. I feel him grow thicker and harder inside me. My lips part as his fingers slide back to ease my ache. "Oh, God, yes." I barely recognize my own desperately needy voice.

He growls and thrusts hard. A light flashes behind my eyes. He's pounding into me, and I'm out of my mind, out of control, soft cries escaping, everything in me coiling tight even as he pushes me open with his deep thrusts.

I scream as I come apart, shudders racking my body as pleasure breaks over me in an endless wave.

"Yesss," he hisses before gripping my hips with both hands and thrusting hard and fast. Pleasure bursts through me with every thrust, and then he lets go with a long low groan.

I try to catch my breath, my eyes closing, exhausted and shaky.

He gently slides my ankles off his shoulders and pulls out. My legs feel jittery as I lie there, limp. The mattress shifts as he gets out of bed. A few moments later, he's back, sliding under the covers. He pulls me toward him so we're lying side by side, chest to chest. I snuggle in close to his heat, throwing an arm and a leg over him.

He strokes my hair back. "How do you feel?"

"Fucking amazing."

He chuckles. "Good. We fit."

"Barely."

He tips my chin up, his eyes dancing with amusement. "Are you trying to tell me I'm hung like a horse?"

"Maybe it's just been a while for me."

He nips my lower lip. "Probably both."

"No complaints in that department." I smooth a palm over his chest, loving the hard play of muscle. "It was intense the first time way back when and even more so now. You think it will get more intense every time?"

"It's intense because we work. As long as we keep working, hell yeah, it'll be intense. That's why I bolted the first time. I'd never felt anything like it."

I still. "Really? That's why you bolted? I thought you got what you wanted, so you left."

"*You* got what *you* wanted, and I got the worst case of *gotta get my fix* for months after that. What was I supposed to do, follow you out to California to college?"

"Yes!"

He kisses my forehead, my nose, and then my lips. "It wasn't the right time. I knew you needed to focus on college, and I'd just be holding you back. I never thought you'd marry right out of college and stay there."

"I can't say I regret my choices. I felt good about them at the time." I snuggle into his chest and sigh. "But things didn't turn out like I thought, and sometimes life is rough."

"Truth." His arm tightens around me. "Stay the night."

I smile. "Kinda feels like I have to with the grip you have on me."

He loosens his grip, cupping the back of my neck and kissing me gently. "I meant to take my time with you. Stay the night, and I'll show you slow and thorough."

I laugh, a giddy happy laugh. "I don't think I'll survive it. This was plenty slow and thorough. I was out of my mind."

He doesn't smile back, his expression intense. "Did you get out of your mind with your ex?"

"Never."

His hand strokes down my spine before cupping my ass. "Good answer."

"It's the truth."

"I didn't mean for this to happen so soon. I thought we'd talk for a while."

"It's hard to fight chemistry. I'm glad we just went for it. I haven't felt this good in a really long time."

He gets quiet, stroking up and down my back. Somehow it soothes me and excites me at the same time. It's all tied to the weird dynamic we have of knowing each other yet not. Familiar yet new.

"We know we're compatible in bed," he says.

"Yup."

"Next step is to see if we're compatible living together."

I prop up on an elbow. "You really want me to move in?"

"Seems like the next logical step before marriage and baby. Two months or so, and we should know if it'll work."

Reality creeps in, making my heart pound and my mind race. Somehow it all feels different now. Real. Like a relationship. Wait. "Isn't that just the natural course of a relationship?"

One corner of his mouth lifts. "Natural course is drinks, dinner, dating, sex, moving in, marriage, kids. You started with kids, and I had to work us backward from there." He gives my ass a light swat, and I squeak.

I refocus on the alarming speed of this relationship. "You're racing through the steps, though."

His blue eyes sparkle. "Well, your eggs aren't getting any younger."

I smack his shoulder, and he grins, rolling on top of me and nuzzling into my neck. I sigh and wrap my arms around him. I'm not used to so much physicality, but I'm starting to appreciate it. He nips and kisses his way up my neck, and I shiver. I feel his smile against my neck before he trails hot open-mouthed kisses up to my ear.

I play with the soft thick hair at the nape of his neck, desire stirring within me. How does he do that so easily?

He lifts his head. "Bring as much of your stuff as you want. Make yourself at home. We'll see how we do, eh?"

I still. I'm sure I want a baby soon. I'm not sure I'm ready for this kind of commitment so soon.

"I won't drive you nearly as crazy as your parents," he says before kissing me for so long I melt into the mattress. He shifts, kissing along my collarbone and then lower, his large hand cupping my breast and lifting it to his mouth.

I stop breathing as his eyes meet mine, his lips brushing across my painfully tight nipple. "I've never lived with a woman before." His words run hot over my skin. "I'm making an exception for you because you're so damn sexy."

I tug his hair and arch my back, needing his mouth on me.

"Ariana, tell me what you're thinking right now."

"I need you so bad. I need your mouth on me, your hands on my skin, your cock deep inside me."

"Fuck. I need that too, baby." He shifts upward, propping himself on his forearms over me. "But I need to know how you feel about moving in."

I search his features, and he seems utterly calm. He's ready to settle down. I swallow hard, dropping my hands from him. "I'm scared. It seems fast."

"It's fast, and it's not. We've known each other a long time. I missed my chance with you once, and I don't want to miss it again. I want to be part of that family you want to get started on."

"How could you want that?"

"I just do."

Adrenaline races through me, and I shift my gaze over his shoulder as a riot of emotions tumble through me. I want him. I want a baby. I want to take a risk because it could all be worth it. This out-of-control racing to a relationship was all my doing because I'm the one who brought up him being my baby daddy. I can't seem to separate the two in my mind now. My longing for a baby and Dylan as the father. I just have to get myself in gear. Risk my still-healing heart. There's no baby until I commit to him anyway. He made that clear. Oh, God. My mouth goes dry.

I could still keep a foot out the door.

I could walk away even right now. I don't have to spend the night. If I pushed him off me, he'd roll with it. Except he feels too good to push away.

His big hand holds my jaw, bringing my gaze back to his, and I'm mesmerized by the intensity of his expression, a fierceness that takes my breath away.

His voice is a rough growl. "I told you before I'll keep you safe, and I meant it. You don't need to be scared. I'll protect you at any cost, even from myself."

I blink, my tension easing a bit at his fierce protectiveness. "Oh." It's all I can manage.

"Wrap your arms around me if you're on board."

My arms obey before my mind can protest. And then his mouth's on mine, and I'm lost, drowning in sensation. He takes control once more, and my body accepts what my heart can't. I'm his.

$$9$$

Ariana

When I get home the next morning, I pack one small suit-case. It's enough to last me a week. I tell myself it'll be like a vacation. One week in the foreign land of Dylan, and then I can come back. Now for the difficult part, breaking the news to my parents. They're of the mind that people shouldn't live together before marriage because it's "playing house" and flaunting premarital sex, which is not cool with our religion. It's hard to keep up with what's a sin or not around here. I mean, I did get the go-ahead for a sleepover. Not that I need their permission.

It's late Saturday morning, which means Ma has made a full breakfast, and they're eating it together. I do take hope from their example. They enjoy each other's company. Ma is fiery and full of energy; Dad is laid-back and mellow. It works.

I set my suitcase by the front door and head back to the kitchen. "Morning."

"Good morning," my father says.

"I take it your time with Dylan went well," my mother says with a big smile.

I fight back a blush. "Very well. Thanks." I get a plate and help myself to blueberry pancakes, scrambled eggs, and bacon. I love Saturday morning breakfast.

I take a seat at the table and dig in. I'll broach the subject of me living with Dylan for a week or so after I finish eating. I don't anticipate it being an easy conversation.

I can feel their eyes on me.

I jump up and get myself a cup of coffee and a tall glass of water. As soon as I sit down again, my mother says, "So, it seems it wasn't just a business dinner. Now don't you wish you wore a skirt?"

I chew and swallow. "It was business, but we got to talking, ya know, catching up on old times."

My parents exchange a knowing look. Oops. I forgot they know what went down in old times.

I take a sip of coffee. "I'm going to be a consultant for his business. He's CEO now and wants to branch out from construction to real estate development."

"You got a job! Congratulations!" my father says.

My mother glares at him. "Now she's complicated things. She can't work for him and date him." She turns back to me. "Why would you muddy the waters like that? I thought your goal was a baby, which means a husband."

"He asked me to," I say and go back to eating. I don't mention that I'm working for free in exchange for his cooperation in other areas. My mother is a ticking time bomb, and I'd like to enjoy this last home-cooked meal before she explodes.

"It's good news, Donna," my father says to my mother. "She has a stellar education. She should use it."

"I know she's got brains," my mother says. "She's a smart girl, but now it's complicated. There are workplace rules. Haven't you heard of the hashtag me too movement?"

My head jerks up. My mother knows about that? I didn't even think she knew what a hashtag was. She must sense my surprise because she turns to me. "Yes, your mother is with the times. You think your generation owns the digital age? I'm plugged in."

I lift a palm. "That's awesome, Ma." She's in her fifties, but she's so old school I didn't think she enjoyed the internet. She's more about church, volunteering at the children's room in the library, and serving on the school board.

She harrumphs and gets up, clearing her dishes and heading to the sink. My father sips his coffee and says nothing.

I finish up my meal while my mother cleans the kitchen in her efficient way. My father helps by drying the dishes and putting them away. They've got a system.

I get up to clear my dishes. My mother takes them from me before I can rinse them, and does it herself. I lean against the counter, take a deep breath, and spill my guts. "So I've got good news. Besides just having a new consultant job, I'm also moving into Dylan's place. We're just gonna try it out, ya know, see if we're compatible." At my parents' twin looks of surprise—eyes wide, jaws slack—I barrel on. "He's ready to settle down, and I'm willing to give it a try."

"When?" my father asks.

"Today."

"Trying it out?" my mother bursts out, her hands gesturing wildly. "You were supposed to bait the hook not throw yourself in the net!"

I don't even know where to start with that one.

"Living in sin!" she exclaims to my father. He looks to me and back to her, seeming unsure where he's supposed to stand on this issue.

"It's not a sin, Ma."

"Oh, yes, it is." She thrusts a hand toward my dad. "Your father and I never lived together. It was courtship and then marriage. That's the way it's supposed to be. Right, Tony?"

"Times have cha—" my father starts.

She cuts him off. "Tell that to Father Richards."

I keep my voice level. "I'm sorry you feel that way, but—"

She lifts a finger. "I bet Dylan's mother will *not* be happy about this news, and I'm gonna tell her!" She marches out of the kitchen.

"Ma! Wait!" I race after her.

She surprises me by going upstairs, so I follow her. She

goes to the bathroom, brushes out her hair, and swipes lipstick across her lips. She taught me never to leave the house without lipstick.

I catch her eye in the mirror. "You're actually gonna talk to Mrs. Rourke for the first time in years over this?"

She turns from the mirror. "You'll understand when you're a mother. And I hope you have a daughter just like you." She says it like a curse.

"Me too."

"Fresh," she huffs before marching downstairs.

I follow her. "Exactly what do you plan to say to his mother?"

"The horrendous truth."

"I'm going with you."

"Suit yourself."

I have the urge to check my hair and makeup, but there's no time. I haven't seen Mrs. Rourke face-to-face since I was a girl, and now she could be my mother-in-law very soon. I want to make a good impression. Somehow I think that ship has sailed with the arrival of my mother.

My mother rings the bell next door and waits, chin in the air, red-painted lips pressed into a straight line.

Mr. Rourke answers the door. I get a flash vision of him and Mrs. Rourke going at it on the sofa from Dylan's detailed story, which I banish quickly to the dark recesses of my mind. Instead I focus on the fact that Dylan looks a lot like him, except his father has gray at his temples, some lines around his eyes, and his eyes are a striking aquamarine color. His posture is regal though, shoulders back, head high, proud and dignified. I could see him as royalty now. My expectations of who he was, based on his occupation, colored my view. Of course, I was just a kid when I last saw him. He was the dad next door who worked in a construction office. Not so different from any of my working-class neighbors.

His brows draw together. "Good morning. Is everything okay?"

My mother shakes her head. "Unfortunately, it's not. Is Tara home?"

"You want to speak to Tara?" he asks in clear surprise and then immediately steps back. "Come in, come in. I'll get her. She's upstairs getting ready."

He invites us to have a seat in the living room, but my mother refuses to sit. Instead she stands in the front hall. I take the offered seat on a plush dark blue sofa.

"Good to see you again, Ariana," Mr. Rourke says. "I heard you were back home."

"Thanks, you too."

He pauses like he wants to ask me a question. Probably, what the hell is going on with your mother? But then he seems to think better of it and heads upstairs.

A few minutes later, I hear both Mr. and Mrs. Rourke downstairs, so I join everyone in the small front hall.

"Is something wrong with Tony?" Mrs. Rourke asks my mother right away. That's my dad.

"No, he's fine," my mother says tightly.

Mrs. Rourke turns to me. "Hello, Ariana. Good to see you." Dylan got her piercing blue eyes. She's quite beautiful, with straight shoulder-length dark brown hair, smooth fair skin, and those striking eyes. She's fit with a vitality that makes her seem younger than her fifties. Probably helps that she dresses casually in a soft-looking white V-neck sweater and black skinny jeans. I hope I look that good after having kids. And she had six of them!

I smile. "You too."

Her brow furrows as she turns back to my mother, who is practically vibrating with tension. "Can I get you something to drink?"

"No, thank you," my mother replies tersely. "We need to talk."

"Okay, why don't we get comfortable in the living room." She shoots Mr. Rourke a significant look, and he joins us.

My mother sits in the center of the sofa and I sit next to her. Mr. and Mrs. Rourke take the adjacent matching love seat.

"It's been a while," Mrs. Rourke says. "How are you and your family?"

Total understatement, and very gracious of her to try to ignore my mother's tenseness. She's smoothing things over.

My mother leans forward. "Are you aware of what is going on with our children? Dylan and Ariana intend to play house."

Mrs. Rourke's eyebrows shoot up. "I'm sorry, I don't understand."

My mother throws her hands in the air. "They're living in sin! At his place! Now I ask you, how can she find a husband like that? He'll never marry her. Why would he when he's got everything he wants from her, if you know what I mean."

Mrs. Rourke's eyes widen. "This is the first I'm hearing about it. I didn't even know they were dating." She turns to Mr. Rourke. "Did you know?"

"News to me," he says.

"How can this be?" Mrs. Rourke asks. "Ariana, didn't you just get home around Christmas? It seems fast. You've only been home for, what, three weeks?"

"We're just testing our compatibility by living together," I say. "Maybe it won't work out. Better not to waste time and know that early on. We're being practical."

Everyone stares at me, so I keep going. "Dylan and I have a history. We know a bit about each other already."

"A bit?" my mother and Mrs. Rourke say in unison.

"It's wrong," my mother tells Mrs. Rourke. "They're living in sin, and no good can come of it."

Mrs. Rourke studies me for a moment. "Aren't you recently divorced?"

"Six months ago!" my mother exclaims. "And separated before that. She's ready to start a family. You understand why I'm upset. How can we ever expect to get a grandchild if they're just playing around? This is wrong, wrong, wrong. It's courtship, marriage, then grandchildren."

They both eye me, and I suddenly wish Dylan was here to explain himself. This was *his* idea to test our compatibility by living together. I would've been fine with a sperm donation. But no-o-o, Dylan doesn't want any part of that. He wants something real. He's the one who invited me back to his place and…my mind drifts. Last night was really, really nice. The glorious heat and weight of him, his big hands holding me, his blue eyes sparkling as he smiled at me. He has a really nice smile. I never saw it much before. I made him happy. My chest expands with pride. I really like that I made him happy.

Mr. Rourke speaks up, his voice ringing with crisp authority. "They're adults."

Mrs. Rourke gets up to sit on the sofa on the other side of my mother. "I understand your concern, Donna. It's too fast."

My mother nods. "It's a bad beginning and doomed to fail. No good can come of it, and my Ariana wants a baby. That's the whole reason she got a divorce. Her idiot ex didn't want kids. He stole her youth, I tell ya! Now she's thirty-one with dusty eggs and so desperate she's looking at binders of anonymous men! Do ya think I want a lunatic's genes in my family?"

Mrs. Rourke blinks for a few moments and glances at me.

I lift my palms. "I was considering a sperm bank." With the perfect donor all picked out.

"And now you're considering Dylan?" Mrs. Rourke asks, zeroing in on a truth I'm not ready to share.

"I've put the sperm bank on hold to see how things work out with Dylan," I say, which is the truth.

Mrs. Rourke turns back to my mother. "I'm still a little bit in shock. Dylan has never made a commitment like this before."

"What commitment?" my mother retorts. "He's getting the milk for free with my daughter being sacrificed as the cow of his convenience!"

"Ma, I'm not a cow!"

"Ariana, this is between me and Mrs. Rourke." She turns back to her new ally. "I want grandchildren, and I'm sure you do too."

Mrs. Rourke's eyes go soft. "I do." She lowers her voice and leans toward me. "The men in the Rourke family are virile. I got pregnant bim-bam-boom, six boys."

Mr. Rourke stands and walks out of the room, shaking his head. The mothers don't even notice his absence, speaking in a hushed tone about age and fertility, and why do young people wait so long nowadays?

I clear my throat. "Good talk. Ma, we should go."

She ignores me, telling Mrs. Rourke, "We may have to help things along for our shared goal."

Mrs. Rourke gives my mother's arm a squeeze. "I couldn't agree more."

I stare at them, sitting close, united in the grandbaby cause. Is the war over? All it took was a shared goal? Amazing!

Mrs. Rourke leans around my mother to address me. "Ariana, we'd love to have you and Dylan over for dinner."

"Oh, thank—"

"I want them over for dinner at my place," my mother says.

Mrs. Rourke nods. "You take Saturday night dinner, and we'll take Sunday."

My mother bristles. "Sunday is the better night for family dinner. Everyone knows that."

"How about we all go out to a restaurant on Sunday?" Mrs. Rourke suggests.

My mother waves that away. "Too hard to get a table for so many people."

"Just the six of us."

"Dontcha think you should invite the whole family?" my mother asks. Then she lowers her voice, but I still catch "intervention."

I cut in. "Why don't you all come to Sunday dinner at Dylan's place?"

Mrs. Rourke gives me an encouraging smile. "You mean to say *our* place, right?"

Trying it out. I paste on a smile.

My mother relaxes and turns to me. "That's not a bad idea. What should I bring? I could make my three-pepper salad."

Mrs. Rourke chimes in. "Dylan really likes this Greek salad I make."

"Greek!" my mother exclaims. "Bah! What do you, an

Irish Catholic girl, know about Greek food? No, I'll make my—"

"I'll cook everything!" I burst out.

Both women stare at me.

My mother breaks the silence. "Did you learn to cook out in California and neglected to help your mother here in New York?"

"I knew your cooking would be superior, so I just enjoyed that," I say.

My mother preens, smoothing her hair, and smiling smugly.

I stand. "Okay, it's settled."

My mother stands too, and I nearly sag in relief. This horrendously embarrassing meeting is finally over.

"I'll bring dessert," my mother says.

"I got it," I insist. "Just bring your smile."

"What a sweet girl," Mrs. Rourke says, smiling at me.

"I know," my mother says. "She takes after her father that way." She nods once. "Tara, thank you for welcoming me into your home. I will see you tomorrow night for our mutual goal."

Oh. I hadn't meant this Sunday. Ah, hell. Let's just get it over with.

Mrs. Rourke smiles warmly. "I look forward to it."

My mother heads toward the door. I say a quick goodbye and follow her. I suppose it could've been worse. She could've done battle with Mrs. Rourke instead of joining forces. Or they could've called for the priest. They go to the same church.

Just when I think we're in the clear, my mother throws over her shoulder to Mrs. Rourke, "Ariana will see the light. I've raised her right."

I wince. There's just a hint of *you didn't raise your son right* in there.

"Same with Dylan," Mrs. Rourke returns pleasantly. "This wasn't his idea. He's never lived with a woman before."

My mother stiffens.

"Let's go, Ma," I urge in a low voice.

She ignores me and whirls. "Your son took my daughter's virginity. In my house! Don't tell me this wasn't his idea. He got a taste of the milk and now he wants the rest for free. Not on my watch!"

Mrs. Rourke's eyes widen. "What? When did this happen?"

"Ya see," my mother says smugly, "that's how sons are. They keep ya in the dark. Daughters tell you everything. Have a talk with your son, Tara. You'll see what's what." She strides out the door, looking pleased she got the last word.

I don't dare look back at Mrs. Rourke. Nothing can take me back to my embarrassing youth like my mother.

"Bye, Ariana," Mrs. Rourke calls. "I do hope things work out. Dylan's a good man, even if he does come off a little gruff sometimes."

I turn back. "I know. Thank you."

Then she surprises me, rushing forward and giving me a hug. She whispers in my ear, "I don't think it's sinful. I think it's a step in the right direction. I've been wanting him to settle down with a nice girl. Don't tell your mom I said so."

I laugh, and she grins at me, her eyes dancing with amusement.

I head out the door feeling a lot better. Now I just have to tell Dylan to prepare for the invasion.

10
———

Dylan

I meet Ariana on the sidewalk in front of my building, expecting a car full of her stuff to haul inside. Instead she springs out of the car, pops the trunk, and pulls a small red wheeled suitcase out. Like you'd take for a weekend trip.

"That's it?" I ask. "You fit two months of stuff in there?"

"I can do laundry."

Odd. In my experience, women have a lot of stuff, even on a weekend trip. One of my exes used to pack multiple outfits and pairs of shoes so she'd have "options" when she was away. Then it occurs to me that maybe Ariana left her stuff behind in California with her old life. I won't bring it up since I know her divorce is a sore subject. I'm selfishly glad for it though. I thought I'd never get the chance to be with her again.

I take her suitcase, swipe my security key, and open the door for her. "We'll get you a key on Monday when the business office opens."

She nods, her expression tight. Is she having second thoughts?

I wait until it's just the two of us on the elevator, after a couple of people get out on the sixth floor, before asking, "How'd your parents take the news that you're moving out?"

She grimaces and says deadpan, "They couldn't be happier."

"Is it because they haven't forgiven me for the earlier, uh, indiscretion?"

She presses a hand to her forehead. "My mother says we're living in sin."

"Old school, huh?"

She drops her hand. "Yes."

"What's the big deal? She already knows we did the deed thanks to your eighteen-year-old confession. How is this any different?"

"I don't pretend to understand how her mind works. All I know is she's sure we're doing this all wrong by living together, and she marched next door to tell your mother so."

My brows shoot up in surprise. "She actually spoke to my mother?"

"Yes! Our misdeeds finally brought them together in a united cause."

The elevator doors open, and I gesture for her to go ahead, and follow her to my door. "Which is what exactly? To make us not live together? How much can they really do?"

She jabs a finger at me. "Underestimate my mother at your own peril."

I let her in and set her suitcase in my bedroom. She doesn't follow, so I retrace my steps and find her in the kitchen, where we came in, with her hands clasped tightly together. Her expression is tight, her entire body tense.

I pull her hands apart and hold them. "Relax. We're adults. We can do what we want."

Her expression is grim. "Both of our families will be here Sunday night for dinner. As in, *tomorrow* night."

I still. "Why?"

"Because they think we're doomed by living together so soon, and they have to fix things if they ever want grand-children."

"My mother said that?"

"Actually, your mom confided to me on my way out that

she thought us living together was a step in the right direction. That was nice of her. She also said I was sweet."

I wrap my arms around her waist with a grin. "Clearly, she doesn't know you very well."

She pouts. "I am sweet."

I dip my head, kissing her until she relaxes against me, her fingers clutching my shirt. I suck her lower lip. Its fullness always tempts me. "You taste sweet, but, deep down, you're a spiky, bloodthirsty woman."

"Spiky," she echoes.

"Yeah, all bite with no warning growl."

Her brown eyes flash, and she pulls away. "First, my mother calls me a cow, and now you compare me to a dog?"

"Come on, a cow is much worse. How're you like a cow?"

She gestures wildly. "Because you don't buy the cow when you can get the milk for free!" At my confused look, she goes on. "It's about sex. Why would you *ever* marry me if you can have me at home giving you the sex whenever you want it?"

I laugh. "The sex?"

"Yes! That's how she thinks! Gah! I sound like my mother now. I swear I will be so chill as a mom. She says she hopes I have a daughter like me, and I hope so too."

"She really got you worked up."

She throws her hands in the air. "She seems to have that effect!"

I take her hand and pull her close again. "I don't think you're a cow at all, or a dog. You're a lioness, fierce and strong."

"Oh." She relaxes and looks up at me. "I kinda like that."

I wrap her hair around my fist and tug, exposing her throat. I pause long enough to see the pulse in her neck quicken before kissing along the side of her neck. I loosen my hold to whisper in her ear, "I love having a lioness in my bed."

Her voice is breathy. "Dylan."

I hold her jaw, stroking her cheek with my thumb. "Yeah?"

She licks her lips, her gaze heated, her skin flushed.

"We're supposed to be testing our living-together compatibility, not just bedroom compatibility."

"How do you feel about the kitchen?"

I lift her to the kitchen island, nudge her legs apart, and step close, spearing my hand through her hair. Her lips part, and that telltale pulse point in her neck beats fast. I place my thumb over it, curling my fingers around the side of her neck. I've got her now.

I kiss her roughly, and she moans deep in the back of her throat. I can't get enough, and I realize she's got me hooked in good. All I can do is go along for the ride for as long as it lasts.

Ariana

Dylan says we should make it easy on ourselves and just order in food for our big Sunday dinner/insane family intervention. But I'm the one who invited everyone over, so I feel like I have to make an effort. We're the hosts. Problem is, I can only make a good sauce and ravioli. It's Sunday morning, and we just got back from the grocery store down the block. I drop my purse in the living room while he carries the groceries into the kitchen single-handedly and sets them on the counter. He's such a take-charge muscleman. There's something deep down in me, buried below all my natural independence, that really digs the way he just takes over and gets things done. A natural leader. Primal drives at work here, because I like it way more than I thought I would.

"So you really think three bags of frozen ravioli is better than takeout?" he asks.

"It's what I can do." I start emptying bags, tucking the frozen food away first.

He shakes his head, smiling. "When you said you could make ravioli, I thought you meant the homemade kind."

"I cook it. It's frozen and then I drop it in the boiling water. Twelve to fifteen minutes later, it's cooked." I shut the freezer door and go for the refrigerated items.

"Okay, now don't take offense, but—" he pulls out his phone "—I'm ordering a six-foot sub and a few cold salads. You can't feed my brothers just frozen ravioli."

Yup, our mothers invited *everyone*, even my sister's entire family in New Jersey, but they couldn't make it since they had a basketball championship to go to for my oldest niece. Shockingly, every single one of Dylan's brothers promised to be here. I think they want to witness the embarrassment. Sean saw my mother in action as chaperone on school field trips and knows the deal.

I park a hand on my hip. "Your brothers will turn their noses up at cooked ravioli from a bag?"

"No, they'll snarf it down and still be hungry." He talks into the phone, placing the order to be delivered later, and hangs up. "I'm still unclear why they were invited. Aren't our parents plenty?"

Since I finished with the refrigerated items, I take a seat on an island stool and watch as he puts stuff away in a small pantry. "Oh, didn't you know? My mother sees this as an intervention of sorts. Need the whole family for that."

He winks. "Don't worry, I'll handle her."

"Ha! You think that, but it'll never work. She'll run circles around you."

"I'm a master at handling women, all ages."

I open my mouth and shut it again. His way of handling me leaves me breathless. I can't help but flash to yesterday right here on this island, where I lost my mind and every inhibition I ever had. *Jesus.* What he does to me.

He cups the back of my neck and kisses me. "Can't argue with that, can you?"

"You can't handle my mother the way you handle me."

"I have manners. That's all she needs to be eating out of my hand. Unlike you, dirty girl."

I'm too distraught over tonight to even smile at his teasing. Instead I rest my elbows on the island and drop my head in my hands. He rubs my back. "I can't believe we have to justify ourselves to our entire family. I mean, yes, it's fast, but can't they just let us see what happens on our own?" I can't exactly defend the relationship other than to say that Dylan has promised me a set course to a family, and I'm willing to give it a chance because I like him. A lot. He's fantastic father material, has great genes (royal too!), and he's good to me. Not just in bed. Well, we've mostly been getting naked, but even then he takes care with me like I'm special.

I straighten suddenly in alarm. *Am I falling for him already?*

Before I can freak out, he turns me toward him and kisses me.

I pull back. "I'm having a bit of a crisis. Can you give me a sec?"

"Yup."

He watches me carefully, and then I feel silly sitting here lost in my panicky thoughts. I stand. "Let's do something fun today before the intervention."

"My thoughts exactly."

"I'll get my purse."

I head for the living room and yelp in surprise when he grabs me by the waist and tosses me over his shoulder. The breath whooshes from my body. He caresses my bottom and a rush of heat floods me, and then I go limp because I know he's got me, and there's nothing I need to do or think right now.

"Look at that," he croons, "you're relaxing already."

"I am." I don't mind admitting it because I like when he carries me. I even like when he surprises me with his grabs and affectionate touches because it gets me out of my head, which is sometimes a stressful place to be.

He carries me to the bedroom and gently sets me down in the center of his king-sized bed.

I open my arms to him. He kicks off his shoes and joins me, reaching out to my shoulders. I squeak as he flips me onto my stomach, surprising me again. He rubs his hands down my back, giving my ass a squeeze with both hands before spreading my legs and sliding a warm hand between them. I close my eyes, the rush of pleasure rendering me speechless.

He shifts to lift my hair and kiss the nape of my neck

gently. I sigh and sink into the mattress. His big hands then proceed to massage me from neck to toes. I'm so grateful I almost blurt, "I so want to have your babies!" But it's too close to our potential future, so instead I moan into the pillow in pure bliss.

By the time he finishes the massage, I'm so relaxed I'm drunk with it. He rolls me over and pulls me to sit up, and I merely smile what I'm sure is a goofy smile. He strips me out of my clothes with no help from me and proceeds to kiss and touch me from my neck to my toes. It doesn't even tickle my toes. Everywhere he touches sparks fire across my skin.

He levers himself back up my body and holds my jaw with one large hand. "You know what I like about you?"

"What?"

"Your complete surrender. You just relax and let go."

"Only with you," I say softly.

"Why is that?" He nuzzles into my neck, and I tilt my head to give him better access.

"Because…I dunno."

He lifts his head. "Tell me."

"You're strong, so I don't worry you'll drop me, and I feel safe with you, so I don't worry about what you're going to do." He grunts in approval of my assessment. He told me I'm safe with him a few times now, so I know it's important to him. A surge of affection rushes through me because he managed to do the impossible and make intimacy possible for me. "I know whatever you do, I'll love it."

He cups my cheek. "You *are* sweet. How did I miss this?"

"I told you I was sweet. Now strip."

His eyes flare with heat. "I want you waiting for me on all fours. I'm gonna make you forget everything but my name."

My breath comes harder, my pulse rushing through my veins. "I want that."

A slow sexy smile dawns. "I know you do." He eases himself off me and stands to strip next to the bed. I start to watch, but he jerks his chin at me.

I get into position as he asked.

"Beautiful," he says in a hoarse voice. "Spread your legs more. I want to see how ready you are for me."

I hear the rustle of the condom as I do as he asks. He mutters a curse, and then suddenly he's right there, covering me, guiding himself in place. I lift my hips in silent invitation and am quickly rewarded with his hard thrust. He kisses my shoulder before thrusting again. I push back into him, needing more. Oblivion. I want the dark oblivion of pleasure he brings me.

His voice is gravelly. "You like it when I fuck you hard, don't you, dirty girl?" He thrusts hard again, and I stutter out a yes.

"You know what I like?" he whispers in my ear, his hand sliding to pleasure central.

"Me?"

"Yeah, Ariana, you, shuddering under me, losing control. You want me to take you there, out of your mind, begging?" He does a slow roll with his hips that brings a rush of pleasure straight up my spine, and then he gives me a sharp tap with his fingers that makes my entire body jerk.

"Yes," I whisper. "Take me."

He squeezes the nape of my neck as he slowly pumps into me. My cheek lowers to the pillow, my breath shuddering out.

He takes and takes and I give with full abandon, trembling under him as he thrusts hard and deep, his fingers wicked, drawing me closer and closer to the edge. The room dims in my vision, the pleasure so sharp I'm panting and drenched in sweat. His fist wraps in my hair, pulling me up so my back touches his chest as he pumps into me. I grab the headboard for leverage. His teeth sink into my shoulder. Harder, faster, dizzying heights. I cry out as the orgasm explodes through my body. He swears as he pumps into me roughly, his fingers closing over my nipples and giving me a hard pinch that sends me over again in a shock of intensity. He stills, his hands soothing now, gliding over my breasts, down my stomach, and palming me firmly between the legs. I gasp, still sensitive.

"Shh," he says in my ear. "Bringing you back to earth slowly."

I whimper as he caresses me gently, white-hot jolts following every soft touch.

"Once more," he growls and then carries through before I can manage a word.

I go under, drowning in sensation, and then break hard. "Fuck!" I buck wildly against him, but he's got me in a firm hold as pleasure floods my body in a rush. Electric sensation races through my every nerve ending, leaving me panting and tingling all over. He pumps toward his own release and finally lets go with a groan.

"Baby." He pulls my sweaty hair out of my face and turns me for his kiss. "Beautiful." Finally he releases me, and I collapse on the mattress.

He's moving around me, and then he returns to me. "Come take a shower with me. We smell like sex."

"Can't move."

"The water will wake you up."

"Water," I croak.

He takes the hint and returns with a glass of water for me. I sit up and drink until it's gone. "Thanks." I set the glass on the nightstand. "We should probably talk."

He strokes my shoulder. "About what?"

"I dunno. My brain seems to be fried, but isn't that why we're living together? Relationship, communication, trust."

"You trust me in bed."

"I guess."

He grabs me by the ankles and yanks me flat on my back. I don't even manage a yelp. "Spread your legs."

I do, even though I'm sensitive.

He kisses me gently on my still-throbbing sex. "Your trust deserves to be rewarded."

"Dylan, please," I say on a moan. I'm not sure if I'm asking him to stop or asking for more. My body and mind can't agree.

He grins and rises over me. "I'm getting addicted to making you beg."

I run my fingers through his hair, feeling drunk again, my limbs loose, my body buzzing. It's pure euphoria and I never want it to end. "I love the way you make me feel, but we should get to know each other better. What're you thinking about?"

He shifts to speak near my ear, the words running hot over my skin. "I'm thinking how long until I can fuck you again."

I shiver. "That's honest."

"See how good we communicate. Come on. We're getting a shower." He gets out of bed.

Reason returns the moment he stops touching me. I pull the covers over me. I'm not complaining, but we're here for a reason, and it's not just supposed to be sex, sex, sex. "I need some time to think. I'll get one after you."

He sits on the side of the bed. "Think about what?"

"About what we're doing here."

"We're finding out what it's like to live together."

I shake my head. "We're finding out how many times we can fuck in a weekend."

"Love hearing you say fuck." He brushes my lower lip with his thumb and presses on the center. "I'm sure we'll slow down eventually, but why not indulge? You got someplace you need to be?"

I sit up. "I need to know you see me as a person not just a body." He glances at my breasts as the covers fall, and I hike the covers up to my shoulders and hold them there.

He smirks. "But a person is a body."

"There's more, you know, on the inside."

His eyes gleam. "I know."

I drop the covers and scoot around him, stalking to the bathroom. "I can't even talk to you."

"Talking right now, aren't we?"

I throw my hands up. His footsteps thud behind me, and my heart thuds in time as I brace for impact.

11

Dylan

I catch up to her on the way to the en suite bathroom, her full breasts bouncing. I fucking love her spirit. I'm naturally aggressive in bed, and that scares some women off or they get nervous. She's unfazed. All she cares about is the fact that I want to fuck her more than talk to her. Doesn't she see how much I need her? It's an intense craving that won't let go.

I follow her into the bathroom, admiring her ass as she adjusts the water temp. I dive into conversation just to please her while we wait to get to the serious business of getting clean while getting dirty at the same time. "Where do you stand on the toilet situation? Do we keep the mystery and shut the door, or do we just go for it, even if the other person is in here?"

She raises her brows, turning to look at me over her shoulder. "I'd like a little mystery."

"Ah. So bodily functions are behind closed doors. Good to know."

She shakes her head. "I cannot believe we're talking about this."

"Getting to know each other's preferences," I say so she'll know I'm doing that whole getting-to-know-each-other thing she wants.

She steps into the shower, and I follow her in. "Dylan!"

I shift her so she gets more of the warm spray. "What could be more important for living together than to spell out the boundaries?"

"Hello? Boundaries? You're in the shower with me."

"Yeah. We both need to get the sex scent off us before the horde arrives."

"Couldn't you wait until I finish?"

I turn her so her back is to my chest and cup her breasts, pinching her nipples. She moans loudly. "What's the fun in that?"

I clamp my teeth on the cord of her neck, and this time she moans softly. I slide my fingers between her legs to find her hot and wet. From before? From now? Who cares? She's melting against me, her hand gripping my forearm to keep her upright, her head tilting back on my shoulder. I shift, pressing her palms against the wall, and whisper in her ear, "Baby, I think we're not done getting dirty." I wrap an arm around her waist to hold her in place and give her one soft stroke with my other hand. Her knees give out, but I've got her tight. "You with me?"

"Yes," she says softly.

Her soft voice makes me even harder. "I'm going to make you come before I take you," I growl in her ear.

She lets out a shaky breath.

And I do as promised because that's also part of trust.

She's begging me to give it to her, even before I tell her to. I press her down between the shoulder blades, bending her over, and take her to the hilt. She gasps at the deep penetration, and I get harder, fighting for control. *Not yet.*

I stroke her, pumping slow and deep, until she's keening under me, pushing back into me for more. And then I feel her clamp down, her head arching back, and I let go, pounding into her as she goes off with a sharp cry.

I pull out at the last second. No condom. I realized it just in time. I don't know how much that matters to her, but it matters to me. If I have a kid, it's going to have my name, born into a stable family.

I wash off, and she slowly turns, leaning against the wall, her chest heaving. Her skin is flushed bright pink, her eyes closed as she catches her breath. A surge of raw possession goes through me. I pull her close and kiss the top of her head.

She melts against me, leaning into my chest. "I'm so sleepy now. Relaxed."

"Good."

I grab the soap and wash her, rinse her, and then do myself while she watches in fascination. I step out first, drying off and wrapping a towel around my waist. Then I grab a towel from the linen closet, pull her out, dry her off, and wrap her tight.

She smiles. "I feel like I'm in a cocoon."

"Nap or get dressed?" I'm prepared to give her a break if I have to, though I'd rather spend the whole day in bed with her. We could always take another shower.

"A nap sounds great," she says, nearly slurring her words.

I smile to myself. I did good work here. I scoop her up, cradled in my arms. "A lioness always rests before the big event."

"You mean dinner?"

"You'll see."

She gives my arm a light slap. "Dylan! You can't always be thinking about sex. That's very one-track minded of you."

"Only when I have you in my bed."

She sighs. "Are you gonna keep me in bed for the next two months?"

"Nah. I'm gonna move you around a bit. Kitchen counter, the wall, living room sofa. I'm very flexible that way."

"Are we ever gonna talk about real stuff?"

"Sure, whatever you want to talk about."

I set her in the bed, and she rolls to her side, curling up with a sigh. I join her, spooning her from behind and pulling the covers over us.

"I want to ride with you on your bike," she says.

I brush her hair back. "Done."

She turns to look at me over her shoulder. "Why did you call me Airy Fairy?"

"Because you were such a girly girl in your pink tutu, twirling around light as a fairy. I want to see you dance again. It was such a big part of your life for so long."

She turns back and snuggles into me. "I'm too rusty."

"You can be bad at it."

She laughs. "I suppose I could."

She's quiet for so long, I close my eyes. I'm nearly asleep when I hear her soft question.

"Do you care for me?"

"Yes." I wait a beat. "Do you care for me?"

Silence.

"Ariana?" I lean over and see she's sleeping.

I guess that's all she needed to know. No problem. I know she cares for me. She wants me to be her baby daddy, and that's the highest compliment a man could get. It looks like smooth sailing ahead.

It's not smooth sailing ahead. Probably should've seen that coming with our family descending on my place like a swarm of locusts.

Mrs. Bianchi has a gift bag in hand when she steps inside with Mr. Bianchi. My parents arrived just a few minutes ago.

"Hello," Ariana says warmly. "Welcome. You didn't have to bring us anything."

"Welcome," I echo.

Mrs. Bianchi eyes me, shoots a quick look at Ariana, who's glowing from all the orgasms I gave her, and then surprises all of us by thrusting the gift bag toward my mother. "For you, Tara."

"Oh, thank you," my mom says, her brows shooting up. "This is a surprise."

"Open it," Mrs. Bianchi urges. "It's something you've wanted for a long time." She shoots Mr. Bianchi a look. He coughs and looks to my dad, who's just standing there staring at the gift bag.

It's got to be the missing serving spoon. Mrs. Bianchi

wants to end the feud for my and Ariana's sake. But I don't think my mom will appreciate getting it back at this late date.

My mom peels back the white tissue paper and produces a serving spoon. She frowns. "This isn't mine."

Mrs. Bianchi bristles. "Of course it's not yours. Do you think I stole it, kept it hidden in a drawer for decades, and then gave it back as a gift?"

"I don't know what to think," my mom says flatly, dropping the spoon back in the bag.

Ariana sends me a worried look. I lift one shoulder. At least they're talking openly now instead of making broad announcements in front of each other on the street.

Mrs. Bianchi gestures toward the gift. "It's a serving spoon with a Gaelic pattern like you said yours was. I can't say I know the exact pattern since I never saw that spoon in my life."

"You complimented the pattern," my mom says through her teeth.

"Who wants wine?" Ariana asks brightly.

"Great idea!" I say.

"Thank you for the peace offering," my dad says to Mrs. Bianchi. "It's long past time we mended fences."

Ooh, he got in a jab about their broken fence, which let their mutt crap all over our yard for years.

My mom hides a smile.

Mr. Bianchi nods. "We're here for Dylan and Ariana. The rest is water under the bridge." Seems like he missed the jab. Or maybe he's just that nice a guy to let it slide.

I reach for the offending gift bag. "I'll put this with your coat and purse, Mom."

"Thank you, Dylan," my mom says graciously.

"I'll get the wine!" Ariana says, making her escape to the kitchen. I head for the back bedroom to stash the gift bag under her coat.

By the time I get back to the living room with our parents, they're all standing there awkwardly, nobody talking. Ariana must still be in the kitchen pouring wine.

"I'd better give Ariana a hand," I say, making my escape.

"She gets points for trying," Ariana tells me under her breath the moment I reach her side.

"She shoulda let the spoon thing die."

"So should your mom."

I still her hand on the wine bottle and lean in for a kiss. "We're not continuing their insane feud. You and I have more important things to focus on."

She smiles, her eyes soft. "Yes, we do."

She finishes pouring the wine, and I help her carry the glasses in to our parents. After everyone has a glass of wine in hand, they all stare at us like we're going to do something crazy right in front of their eyes. Maybe they're checking for signs of insanity. Ariana did say her mother saw tonight as an intervention. We moved in together after one date. Not so crazy when you've known someone your entire life. Besides, we're both old enough to know what we want. I want her, and she definitely wants me. I can tell I'm growing on her already. She's comfortable with me, letting her guard down more.

"Do you remember what we talked about?" Mr. Bianchi asks me with a hard look.

Ah, hell. The man-to-man talk. Do we all need to hear about that?

"Yes, sir," I say.

Both he and Mrs. Bianchi smile at my manners and exchange a pleased look. I get the feeling they think that talk had a big influence on me or something. I can't say it did, but at the same time, of course I plan to treat Ariana right, so maybe it's all the same in the end.

"What did you talk about?" my mom asks me.

The intercom buzzes, and I jump at the chance to escape once more. "Better get that."

I answer the intercom, and in short order my brothers Sean and Connor arrive. I linger in the kitchen with them. Jack, Brendan, and Garrett show up a short while later. Ariana hasn't come looking for me yet, and I know I should get back in there, but I need a break from parental scrutiny. I'll wait until they're all mellowed a bit from the wine.

"When's the wedding?" Sean asks me with a smirk.

"One date and they're shacking up together," Brendan says, waggling his brows. "We know what that means."

"Shut up," I say, opening the cabinets in search of something for us to snack on. There's a box of crackers. How old are these? I search for the expiration date.

The food I ordered isn't here yet, and Ariana decided to skip the ravioli since she thought it didn't go with a six-foot sub. I told her my brothers will happily eat any combination of food. Their stomachs are bottomless pits. Not an ounce of fat on them either between the hard physical labor of construction and the workouts they do on their own to keep fit. As kids we were all active in sports, and it helped burn off the extra energy kids have.

I toss the crackers in the garbage. They expired six months ago. Guess I haven't cleared out the cabinets in a while.

I turn to them. "Who wants a beer?"

A series of affirmative grunts has me pulling out a six-pack and distributing them. I take a beer for myself and leave my wine untouched on the island. I should probably get back in there with the parents soon. It's just such an awkward situation.

"He's never shacked up before," Connor says as he studies me. "Maybe it's the real deal."

"Or she's pregnant," Brendan says under his breath.

I shake my head. "Can't a guy have his entire family over for dinner the day after his lover moves in without taking shit for it?"

"Yeah," Garrett says. "Maybe it's love."

They crack up.

"Maybe I am in love with her," I snap, and they shut up. "Would that be so bad?" I don't know how else to explain the intensity of our connection. It was that way when we were younger, and it's only multiplied since then.

Strangely, no one busts my balls about my rare admission of feelings. Then I realize they're looking over my shoulder. I slowly turn to find Ariana and Mrs. Bianchi standing right behind me.

Ariana's big brown eyes lock with mine, and the rest of the people in the room fade into the background. The blood rushes through my veins, every nerve ending on alert. This hyper-alive feeling is something I only get when looking into her eyes. It has to be more than chemistry. The hair on the back of my neck rises.

She crosses to me, wraps her arms around my waist and hugs me, her cheek resting on my chest. I hug her back, loving how perfectly she fits against me.

"I'm so happy!" Mrs. Bianchi exclaims. "Love!"

Ariana steps back, and Mrs. Bianchi rushes in to hug me. "Dylan, this is the best news I could've heard today!"

Heat creeps up my neck. This is starting to feel like a public declaration of love. Shouldn't this be a private conversation between me and Ariana? I mean, I said *maybe* I'm in love with her. Doesn't it take time? Maybe I'm only halfway there.

Mrs. Bianchi rushes toward the living room. "Everyone, come in here! Dylan has the best news!"

I debate bolting. My brothers chuckle quietly, clearly enjoying every moment of my embarrassment.

Does it really need to be a family announcement that *maybe* I'm in love with her? Didn't Mrs. Bianchi notice that Ariana didn't say anything back?

"Ma, please," Ariana says, taking my hand and giving it a squeeze. "You're embarrassing him. Let's just talk about something else."

"What's embarrassing about love?" Mrs. Bianchi says with genuine confusion.

I can't help but notice Ariana doesn't look the least embarrassed. Is that because she doesn't feel the same way, or because she's used to her mother doing this kind of thing?

"What's this about love?" my mom asks, a wide smile on her face. She's been saying for years she wants me to find someone special.

My dad and Mr. Bianchi join us. "What's the big news?" Mr. Bianchi asks with a smile.

Mrs. Bianchi points to me. "Tell them, Dylan. Tell them

what you told your brothers. So nice how they share with each other."

I turn to Ariana, standing by my side and not helping in the least. She gives me a small apologetic smile. Obviously, she's not going to take the heat for me. *Thanks, babe.*

I turn back to Mrs. Bianchi, who gives me an encouraging smile.

Okay, let's nip this in the bud. I need to handle Mrs. Bianchi the right way from the start—firm yet polite. Otherwise, she's going to steamroll me.

I clear my throat. "It's no big deal."

"No big deal," Mrs. Bianchi scoffs. "He's being modest. You'll see, Tara, it's just as you said."

"Maybe you're putting him on the spot," my mom says quietly.

"A real man speaks his mind," Sean says in a commanding impersonation of our father.

I barely resist smacking him. Dad was always going on about what makes a man a man. That was one of his many sayings. The rest all had to do with the way you conduct yourself—honor and integrity above all—as well as a lot of irritating etiquette that covered everything from eating to riding in a car. It was the way he was raised and something he thought important to pass on to us. My brothers and I thought it was a huge waste of time and energy, but some of it stuck anyway. Manners, I got 'em, which is why I'm still enduring the torture of my maybe declaration of love in front of way too many people. I won't disrespect Mrs. Bianchi or Ariana. I'm just not sure I can get the words out a second time.

I catch Mr. Bianchi's eye, who shrugs. No help from that quarter. Finally, I think of something I can say without choking on the words. Mr. Bianchi gave them to me earlier in our "man-to-man talk."

"Ariana is special," I say. "Not someone I'd ever treat lightly."

"Okay!" Ariana says. "Moving on to the next part of the evening. Let's talk shop." She turns to my brothers. "Guys, there's a lot of research we need to do scoping out future properties."

But Mrs. Bianchi isn't done. "Dylan, are you embarrassed to finally be in love after all these years? Your mother says it would be the first time for you."

Kill me now. My brothers are grinning like loons. Someone mutters, "Love virgin," under his breath, probably Brendan. This is *not* my first time in love. I don't tell my mother everything. Okay, it's never been this intense before, but—

Mrs. Bianchi goes on. "Honey, don't be embarrassed. It's what we want for you. Now that we know you're in love, it's more likely you'll marry her. Have you talked about it yet?"

"In two months." The words are out before I can think better of them. That was our deal.

Ariana sends me a beseeching look. Shit. I am way out of my element here. I send her a look back that says *fix this!*

"Oh my goodness!" Mrs. Bianchi exclaims. "We need to start planning the wedding right away."

Ariana holds up a palm. "Actually, we're taking it one day at a time. Let's not get ahead of ourselves."

"But he just said—" Mrs. Bianchi starts.

Ariana gives my shoulder a squeeze. "He blurted out the first thing that came to mind because you put him on the spot, but I'm not ready to jump into marriage so soon, which is why we're currently living together."

Silence. A very tense silence.

Mrs. Bianchi frowns and turns to Mr. Bianchi. My parents look uncomfortable. One of my brothers coughs.

Finally, the intercom buzzes and I bolt, pressing the buzzer. It's the food-delivery guy. "Be right down." I head out the door, muttering, "Food's here."

"I'll help you!" Ariana says and collides with me as we both try to get out the doorway at the same time. I let her go first and move swiftly behind her.

We make it to the elevator in record time. I jab the button several times. We take one look at each other and burst out laughing.

"I am so sorry!" she says when she can catch her breath.

"You're not used to a mom with no sense of boundaries. I swear she means well."

"I should've known when she called me your gentleman caller."

"It was worse when I was a kid. I was so shy, and she was forever trying to get me over it in the most embarrassing ways."

The elevator doors open, and we step inside. I hit the button. The moment the doors close behind us, I relax. I glance over at her and can't help but touch, tucking a lock of hair behind her ear. "I didn't know you were so shy as a kid. You were always dancing for the neighborhood to see."

"I was in a dream world when I danced." She smooths her hands over my chest. "My shyness is the only reason I didn't curse you out when you asked where my tutu was. I settled for a death glare."

I laugh. "Just as well. I probably would've found it hilarious coming from a sweet girly girl like you. Now that you're all grown up, I love hearing fuck come out of that sweet mouth. I love that you have claws."

"You're a little twisted."

I cup her cheek and give her a kiss. "I like what I like."

Her hands slide up and over my shoulders, a small smile on her face. She likes touching me. "Your brothers must've been ribbing you pretty hard about me."

"Yeah, well, that's what they do. I'd do the same if it was one of them having an intervention."

She bites her lower lip. "Did you mean what you said, or was that just to shut them up?"

I tip her chin up. "What do you think?"

"I'm asking you."

The doors open, and a young couple gets on, talking about a poetry slam they're heading to.

Ariana pulls away and stares straight ahead.

I lean down to her ear. "Maybe I meant it."

She smiles, a small secret smile that grows into a full smile. "Me too."

A rush of warmth floods me, and I suddenly want to take

her into my arms, but it's not the right time. I have to wait. The doors open, and we get the food from the delivery guy, taking our haul back to the elevator. They cut the sub in half for us ahead of time, but it's still a lot to carry. I press the button with my knuckle, and we head up to the eighth floor, where our entire family awaits.

She gives me a sideways look. "How bad would it be if we pressed the emergency stop and had our own little picnic dinner right here?"

"Bad. Better would be to press the emergency stop, say the hell with dinner, and I take you up against the wall."

Her cheeks flush. "You make me want to do bad things."

"Glad to help." I set the bags of food down. "Now kiss me like you mean it."

She sets her bag down, wraps her arms around my neck, and kisses me passionately. I press her against the wall, taking over the kiss, lust spiking through me.

She breaks the kiss. "I can't believe you're the same man I wanted to throttle all those years ago."

"I can't believe how lucky I am that you chose me all those years ago. You chose me again for your baby daddy. Maybe you always knew I was the man for you in every way."

"Maybe," she says, but her eyes say yes.

My heart swells in my chest. Something deep passes between us, our gazes locked.

The elevator doors open, and she grabs her bag and blows out a breath. "Prepare for round two," she calls over her shoulder on the way out. "And not the dirty kind."

I laugh, scoop up my bags, and follow her. "Figured. At least my brothers' mouths will be too full to say shit about it."

She speaks under her breath. "It's kind of you not to mention my mother's mouth."

"Total respect for the woman who raised you."

She drops her bag and throws herself in my arms. I stumble back and have to drop my bags to right us. She's kissing me, and I guide us back to the wall, leaning against it and pulling her close. She wants me, she maybe loves me, and I'm a lucky man. I wrap her hair around my fist with one hand and cup her ass with the other as the fire ignites between us.

A voice carries into the hall. "Hey, we're hungry in here!"

Ariana pulls away, her cheeks flushed.

Sean crosses to us, grabs two bags, and scowls. "Do that after we leave."

Ariana's fingers go to her lips, her eyes heated on mine. "I'm addicted to your kisses."

Sean groans and goes back inside.

I grin and grab the other bag. "I'm addicted to you."

More of my brothers pop their heads out to see what's holding up the food. I take Ariana's hand, and we rejoin our family, a deeper connection binding us.

Everything is perfect right now. I tell myself to enjoy it, but perfect makes me uneasy. Nothing in my life has ever been perfect for long.

12

———

Ariana

It's been a month since I moved in to Dylan's place. Things are scary good. I keep waiting for the other shoe to drop. Somehow it all clicked into place. He's up early to work out in the gym downstairs; then he showers and heads out to work. He asks very little of me. He just seems happy that I'm here. Truth? I'm happy to be here. I never thought a relationship could be so easy, and I definitely didn't think I'd be ready for one so soon. My ex was very particular, and even the simplest decisions required a lot of back-and-forth and compromise. I thought that was just how marriage was—hard but worth it. Not that Dylan and I are married, but so far it's been pure bliss.

I spend my days busting my butt to help Rourke Management. Mostly I work from home with occasional trips into his office for a meeting with him and his brothers. I've been looking into potential properties to launch the new side of his business, as well as sources of financing. I even got in touch with my former father-in-law to ask him some market-analysis questions. Not an easy thing for me to do, considering my ex's parents knew before I did about Kiersten's pregnancy. They remained sympathetic toward me. Anyway, I toughed out my extreme discomfort for the greater cause. As soon as financing is in place, we'll need to hire more staff. I know Dylan doesn't want to borrow a lot of money, but it could get the ball rolling. He keeps saying he'll figure something out, which I fear means selling the crown and scepter set that are his inheritance. I can't allow that to happen. It's a priceless family heirloom.

My stomach growls. It's almost dinnertime, but I'll wait for him. Usually he gets home a little after five, showers, and then we either order takeout or cook together. Sometimes we don't get to dinner until late because we're so hungry for each other. That is the *only* time he's demanding of me, deliciously so. I don't know where he gets the energy, but I'm not complaining. Nothing is better than the full erotic focus of a man who demands everything and then demands more. By the time he's finished with me, I'm limp and more satisfied than I've ever been in my life. And then he holds me! He strokes my hair, nuzzles my neck, and with every touch I feel the care he takes with me.

I'm in love with him.

I didn't want it to be true. I wasn't ready for it to be true. It just is, and I'm done pretending we're just testing things out. I want a future with him. He was clear from the start that he was ready for a family, and now I can't imagine it with anyone but him.

I'll tell him tonight. Over dinner. Or maybe after sex when he's so loving and the world is a beautiful place.

The moment he steps inside, I meet him in the kitchen and give him a hug. He gives me a quick kiss before pulling away. "Baby, let me shower first. I'm covered in dust and paint."

"I'll join you."

He pinches my chin. "I'm too dirty for you."

"I like your dirty."

He flashes a smile that lights up his face before surprising me, dipping his head and nipping my lower lip. "I'll make you beg later. Now I shower alone."

I pout. "I don't beg."

His blue eyes gleam, his voice gravelly. "You will."

I find myself smiling at his cockiness. "I look forward to it. Should I order us some food?"

"Sure. Whatever you want." He heads toward the bathroom.

See? So easygoing. I call for Thai food and wander into the master bedroom, listening to the shower. He left his phone, wallet, and keys on the nightstand. His dirty clothes are in the hamper, the jeans half out. I tuck the jeans in and sit on the side of the bed to wait. His phone rings, and I lean over to see who it is. His mother. Should I answer it? No. If she wanted to talk to me, she'd call me. I don't think she has my number though.

I hit the button to answer. "Hi, it's Ariana. Dylan's in the shower."

Her voice is low and urgent. "Listen carefully, I only have a minute. Daniel and I are flying to Villroy with the crown and scepter set. Apparently, my husband has been planning this ever since Dylan mentioned selling it. I just found out. He's determined to get what Dylan deserves. Let me know if Dylan can fly to Villroy, and I'll try to hold off a showdown. Ask him to tell his brothers where we are. Oh, and Daniel doesn't want him to know he took the set. Bye."

"Bye," I say to the dead line.

I rub my forehead. Weird. What does Mr. Rourke plan to do with the set in Villroy? Give it back? Demand a place there for his son? Would Dylan actually be a prince? Would he even want that? My head spins with all the possible implications.

Dylan steps out of the bathroom a few minutes later, a white towel around his waist. I'm momentarily dazzled by his incredible physique. His shoulders are rounded with muscle, and there's a tribal tattoo that wraps around his left bicep that makes him look even more badass. His chest is broad and sculpted with muscle from pecs to abs. My gaze follows a light trail of hair that leads to his thick cock. I lick my lips.

His deep voice is low and husky. "I love when you look at me like that, baby."

I jerk my head up. I got distracted by his beauty.

"C'mere," he orders in a commanding tone that has me on my feet. "I'll give you what you need."

I remember myself and sit down again. "Your mom called. I answered your phone since I was here, and she says she and your dad are flying to Villroy."

His brows shoot up. "What? Why? For how long?"

"They're on their way now. I don't know for how long. She said he wants to get what you deserve, and she says you should go out there. She'll try to hold him off."

He grabs his phone and hits a few buttons, listening. Then he tries another number and finally texts rapidly. "Voicemail," he mutters before sinking heavily onto the mattress next to me. "Why would they not tell me ahead of time?"

"Your mom just found out he was going and decided to join him."

He shakes his head. "He hasn't been there since he was exiled more than thirty years ago. Did they invite him?"

"I don't know. Maybe it's a good thing. Maybe he'll finally get what he deserves and give it to you."

"Or they'll say he's already gotten what he deserves. Did he take the crown and scepter with him?"

I hesitate. His dad didn't want him to know he took it, but his mom wants him there, so that means…

"He did," Dylan says. "I can tell from your expression. Shit. What the hell is he planning? I told him I wouldn't sell it until I knew it was okay with him. He said he needed to think on it some more. What's he gonna do, sell it back to his family?"

I lift one shoulder up and down. "I told you everything I know. Oh, and you're supposed to tell your brothers where they went."

He gives my arm a squeeze. "Thanks. Damn. I don't want him to suffer anymore, ya know? Even just visiting Villroy is bound to bring back a lot of painful memories, and I get the feeling he's angling for a confrontation."

"So I guess he felt strongly about not selling it. That means you're back to needing a loan."

"If I can even get one."

"I'll book us on the first flight out, and then we'll come up with a plan together over dinner for financing."

He hauls me into his lap. "You're exactly what I was looking for. A partner to lighten the load."

My heart swells, and I burrow into his bare chest, breathing him in. "I love you."

He tips my chin up, his eyes burning into mine. "Say it again."

My throat tightens, the emotion overwhelming me. "I love you."

He crushes me against him. "I love you too. Love of my life."

My eyes sting. "I think I'm gonna cry."

He holds my jaw. "You can if you want, but I'd rather make you moan." His mouth claims mine, and I'm lost in sensation as his hands roam all over me.

Just then the intercom buzzer sounds. I break the kiss. "Dinner's here."

"Take some money from my wallet and pay the guy."

I stand and salute him. "Yes, sir!"

He grins. "Liking the sir. I'd get dinner, but I'm not dressed."

I stroke his scruffy jaw and give him a quick kiss. "Let's keep it that way. I'm enjoying the view."

Dylan

She loves me. The strange thing is, I wasn't surprised at all. I felt that love in her eyes, in her voice, in her touch. It was more of a relief to hear her say it out loud because it means she's ready to fully commit to me body, heart, and soul. Her body was mine the moment I touched her. Heart and soul peeked at me shyly. Until now.

The only flight we could get on short notice was for tomorrow night, so naturally I stripped her out of her clothes the first chance I got and took her to bed. What can I say, I crave her.

I give her sweet ass a light smack when she gets out of bed. She squeaks, which makes me laugh. I surprise her a lot. I get the feeling her ex was more predictable and probably didn't lift her and touch her as much as I do. I'm a very physical guy, and she has a body that's meant to be appreciated.

She turns and glares at me, and my smile spreads wider. The glaring spitfire, only now she's a full-grown woman who satisfies me in every way.

She jabs a finger at me. "Don't laugh when I squeak."

I hold her finger. "Can't help it. You sound like a little mouse."

"I'm just not used to such a handsy guy."

I hold her by the wrist, brushing my thumb along the sensitive underside. "You like it though."

"Yes," she admits. "But I don't like it when you laugh."

I bite back a smile. "I'll really try not to. How're you feeling?" I pushed her hard this time around. Her throaty moans drove me on.

She gives me a small smile, her eyes lighting up; then she pulls away and does a leaping twirl. "That's how I feel."

Pride surges through me. I've been waiting for her to dance again. "Bravo!"

She dances some more in full ballerina form, her body graceful as her arms lift, her back arching. She does a flying leap before heading into the bathroom with a bounce in her step.

I fold my fingers behind my head and lie back in satisfaction. Her dancing means she's whole again, reclaiming her joy. Our daughters will dance. Hell, maybe our sons too. Why not? A real man makes no apologies for doing what's right for him. Another bit of wisdom from my dad. Oh, shit. Dad's in Villroy and I was supposed to tell my brothers. Can you blame me for getting distracted when I have a sexy woman in my bed who freaking loves me?

I wish my dad would've run this by me. He's setting himself up for another harsh rejection. If he's looking for a trade—cash for the crown and scepter—he'll likely be turned down. You don't show up at the royal palace to return a gift and ask for the cash equivalent. His natural authority could come across as demands. Things will escalate, and their rejection will be like reliving his exile all over again.

He's not thinking straight on this. His own upbringing as heir to the kingdom means he feels my loss more keenly. The only thing I want is to see Rourke Management grow into an empire. He's setting himself up for a boot out the door, and then all hell will break loose. He may have accepted it the first time due to his great love for my mother, but he won't accept being turned away when he's working on my behalf. He has too much guilt over what he thinks he deprived me of.

I grab my phone and send out a group text to my brothers. *Dad's gone to Villroy with the crown and scepter to get some kind of compensation on our behalf. I'm going out tomorrow night to prevent exile part 2, if Mom can hold him back long enough.*

The responses trickle in over the next few minutes, all of them boiling down to WTF.

Connor: *How did he get through security with that hunk of metal? That's got to draw attention.*

Good question. It would be hard to explain why he's carrying around what looks like a valuable museum-quality piece of history. It's even more dangerous to leave it loose for long while security investigates the odd pieces. He couldn't chance putting it in baggage. Unless he flew private. He couldn't afford that, which means the royal jet must've picked him up. My cousin Adrian had offered to fly us out there for the wedding on the jet, but we declined because, well, I guess it was pride.

They had to be expecting him. I'll text Adrian. It's past two a.m. in Villroy, but Adrian's often up late since he works the night shift at his casino. *My dad's heading to Villroy. What's going on?*

No response. Probably busy with casino stuff.

Doesn't my dad see I have it all? I grew up in a loving family, I own my own business, and I found the love of my life. All of it here in Brooklyn. This is where I belong. I need no part of the royalty thing. I've never been happier.

The moment Ariana crawls back into bed, I pull her close, tucking her against my side.

She throws an arm and a leg over me. "I can't believe I'm going to a real honest-to-God palace with my prince tomorrow."

I grin. "Your half-commoner prince, but yeah."

She looks up at me under her lashes, almost shyly. "I'd be like a half princess if I married you."

I kiss her. "You will marry me, and I'll treat you like a full princess."

She blinks a few times and then rolls on her side away from me. I hear a sniffle.

I spoon her from behind, wrapping an arm around her waist and peeking over her shoulder. "Are you crying?"

"Yes, you jerk, stop being such a romantic dream."

I can't help my smile. "I've never been accused of that before you came along."

She sniffles again and wiggles back into me, trying to get closer. My body responds like it's an invitation. I don't think I'll ever stop wanting her. It's insane the way I crave her.

I wait until it seems like she's done sniffle-crying, and then I kiss her neck.

She sighs, tilting her head to give me better access. I take full advantage, her skin heating under me.

She hooks her leg back over mine, opening herself to me. Damn, I love this woman.

I can't believe I'm actually back on Villroy. I never thought I'd see this place again. Ariana has been beside herself the entire trip—the private jet, the yacht to the island, and now the palace courtyard. I heard back from my cousin Adrian, and he arranged all of our travel. We cancelled our commercial flight in favor of the jet. We still had to fly at night our time, but it was a more direct flight to Villroy and way more comfortable. Both Ariana and I slept on the jet. Now it's morning on Villroy, and we're walking through the palace courtyard, heading for the big wooden double doors.

My dad had an entire day here to wreak havoc. I haven't heard from him and only got a quick text from my mom saying she was glad we would be here. Are they too wrapped up in whatever they're doing at the palace? What *are* they doing at the palace? I can imagine my dad working up some imperious speech while my mother urges him to wait for me and give me a chance to speak on my own behalf. I just don't want him to suffer from any more harshness coming from the royal family.

"You really are a prince," Ariana says for the millionth time. "Look at this place. Can you imagine living here?"

I glance around. The palace looks exactly like you think a palace would—sandstone construction with multiple spires and turrets. Not exactly the crowded Brooklyn brick rowhouse I grew up in, though we did live in a nice neigh-borhood.

"No," I say in answer to her question.

"It's so beautiful," she says on a sigh. "Ooh. Go stand by the entrance so I can get your picture."

"No."

I keep walking through the palace courtyard, my duffel bag over my shoulder. My only concern is my dad.

Ariana throws an arm around my shoulders, halting me. Then she snaps a selfie of us with the palace in the background.

"Don't do that again," I growl in my fiercest tone. "I don't want people knowing about my connection to the royals."

"Why? It's cool."

"Because my family was exiled." I pick up her wheeled suitcase from where it fell on its side when she rushed me for the selfie, and continue on while she snaps pictures of the palace. "I don't want any more scandal to follow my dad around."

She catches up to me. "But they invited you back. You're on the inside, baby!"

I halt and narrow my eyes. "You're enjoying this a little too much."

"I'm sure your dad is fine. What're they gonna do, lock him up for demanding his due?"

A trickle of unease goes through me. I hadn't thought of that. This is a kingdom, which means Gabriel and Anna are the law. They have the final word and can do what they see fit, including locking up a threat to their power.

I stride to the large double doors, where two palace guards stand. "I'm Dylan Rourke and this is my fiancée, Ariana Bianchi." I hear a squeak behind me. I already told her she was marrying me, so it shouldn't be a squeaky surprise. "My cousin Gabriel is expecting me." I pull out my passport to show them proof, but they're already waving me through.

We step into the grand entrance hall, and Ariana gasps audibly. "Oh my God, it's stunning!"

I thought so too the first time I saw it. The two-story white marble hall with gilded mirrors and silk wallpaper patterned with gold leaves is meant to impress. But we're here on important royal business—keeping my dad out of the dungeon.

A servant in a dark suit approaches. "I'm Nolan, the butler here at Amalie Palace. Welcome, sir, madam. William will take your luggage. Your room is ready."

Another man in his fifties with a neat comb-over approaches us.

"Thank you, Nolan," Ariana says. "What a beautiful palace you have here."

"Thank you, ma'am."

"I need to see my father," I say. "Can you direct me to him? Daniel Rourke, the former crown prince."

"Yes, of course, we know who he is. My father served him."

"My father too," William says proudly. "I knew Daniel when we were both boys. He was so proper and dutiful, always the height of royal decorum and dignity." He coughs and his gaze shifts to the side. "Until he was swayed in another direction." He means my mother.

I clench my jaw. "He wasn't swayed. He made a choice. Now, please, tell me where he is."

"Sir, you don't want to go there," Nolan says. "May I suggest you meet up for luncheon later."

"I assure you I *do* want to go there," I say through my teeth. "Right now."

Nolan and William exchange a worried look.

"Did they lock him up?" I ask. "Tell me before I tear this place apart."

"Dylan, calm down," Ariana says, squeezing my bicep. "I was kidding earlier about locking him up. It's not like they have a dungeon around here."

William clears his throat. "Actually, ma'am, we do."

"Take me to my father now!" I roar.

"Yeah!" Ariana chimes in. "We didn't come all this way to be given the runaround."

I shoot her a quick look of appreciation and turn to the two servants. Nolan purses his lips. William takes a step back, murmuring, "I'll see to your things."

"Very well, sir," Nolan intones. "Consider yourself warned."

13

———

I swallow hard. "Fine. Just take me to him."

Ariana sends me a worried look as we follow Nolan down a long hallway and up several flights of stairs. A few more twists and turns and we arrive at a closed door. At least it's not the dungeon. That would be under the palace not above.

He knocks sharply. A low bellow and an earsplitting high-pitched scream carry out to the hall like someone is being murdered.

Nolan winces and turns to us. "I don't think he heard me, sir." He opens the door and steps back.

I stare in shock for a moment, trying to figure out what exactly is going on here. My dad is lying flat on his back on the floor, his hair disheveled. A blur of denim rolls off him. A toddler with wild dark curls leaps to her feet. She's barefoot in denim overalls and a yellow polka-dotted T-shirt.

She lifts a small plastic sword from the floor and brandishes it high in the air. "Dead, Pop-Pop!"

Pop-Pop? My dad does a small death struggle and flops still.

I take a quick glance around at the mess of a room. It's a nursery with yellow and white striped walls, a small table with overturned kiddie chairs, and a floor littered with toys, dress-up stuff, and stuffed animals.

"Dad?" He's wearing a purple cape.

My dad's eyes pop open, and he jackknifes upright. "Dylan! You're here!"

"What're you doing?"

He turns to the little girl. "Playing with this little firecracker. Mila, this is your uncle Dylan."

Mila pops her thumb in her mouth and stares at me with big brown eyes, her sword still gripped in one hand.

"Hey, little one, cool sword," I say.

She hides it behind her back like I might take it, still sucking her thumb.

Ariana squats down in front of her. "Hi, Mila. I'm Ariana."

Mila pulls her thumb from her mouth. "Hi."

"Hi!" Ariana says.

"Hi!" Mila echoes with a smile.

I offer my dad a hand up from the floor, but he declines and gets up on his own. He doesn't even fix his messy hair, and he always takes great pride in his appearance. I resist the urge to smooth it down.

"What's going on?" I ask.

My dad beams. "I'm her Pop-Pop."

Mila drops her sword and throws herself at his leg, hugging it. He ruffles her hair, smiling down at her. "She took to me and, since my brother's gone, I'm her honorary grandfather. Kids need a strong male influence in their lives."

I suppose her father the king might be an influence and all of her other royal uncles, but I focus on the more important thing: what the hell he's up to. "Can we talk in the hall?"

My dad takes a step toward the hall, carrying Mila with him on his leg.

"Alone," I say.

"She's attached to me," he says, peeling her off his leg and putting her on his shoulders. She wraps her arms around his head, and he adjusts her hands so he can see.

I turn to Ariana. "Can you play with her?"

She nods. "Mila, I think your dog and bear want to have a tea party. Do you know where I could find teacups?"

My dad sets Mila down, and she points to a mess of toys in the corner.

Ariana goes over to it and holds up a doll-sized shoe. "Is this the teacup?"

Mila laughs and shakes her head.

Ariana holds up a wooden helicopter. "Is this the teacup?"

"No!" Mila exclaims with a laugh and runs over to show Ariana the teacup.

"I'd better hurry before she notices I'm gone," my dad whispers and bolts out the door.

I join him and quietly shut it behind us. He gestures for me to follow, and we head downstairs and into a large suite of rooms. He takes a seat on a beige sofa, and I join him.

"This is Mila's suite with her parents," he says. "She still sleeps in a crib in the room with them." He gestures toward the back of the suite.

I glance around. The king and queen's suite isn't as formal as I thought it would be. We're in a living room area across from a fireplace with a TV mounted above it. There's a round mahogany table with cushioned chairs across the room, parked in front of a large window with a view of the sea. "Where's Gabriel and Anna?"

"They're doing a ribbon-cutting ceremony for an addition to the health clinic. Now that the kingdom is doing better financially, they're rebuilding some infrastructure."

I rest my elbows on my knees. "Okay, so what's your part in all this?"

"I'm really enjoying being a grandfather."

I straighten and work for patience. "Why did you make secret plans to fly here with the crown and scepter?"

"Ah. So your mother told you about that part."

"She told Ariana, who told me. Can you please tell me what's going on?"

"I gave them back," he says. "They belong here."

"And did you ask for anything in return?"

"Well, your mother did her best to get me to wait for you, but I'd waited years to demand what's rightfully mine."

I stifle a groan. "You couldn't wait one more day?"

"This was my duty toward my sons and not your responsibility."

Why did I ever think I could influence him? Why did my mom? He's always been hardheaded and single-minded. On the other hand, he doesn't seem worse for wear. Is it possible his demands were met?

"What exactly did you demand?"

"I asked Gabriel and Anna to contribute toward launching Rourke Management as compensation for everything our family was denied."

I lean back on the sofa, closing my eyes for a moment. I really don't want to take a handout from my cousins. On the other hand, my dad was denied his due. "What did they say?"

"I'll tell you what I said first. I told them with all the righteous indignation that's been burning in my chest for years that I gave my childhood to the crown. My parents brought me up very strictly to do my duty, and then when I wanted to marry the only woman I've ever loved, they cut me off. Exiled with no allowance. They confiscated all of my possessions, some of which were of great value. I left with only the shirt on my back." He pauses, seeming lost in memories for a moment before he focuses back on me. "Gabriel said it was a travesty and he understood my position, but it was their duty to funnel their profits into the kingdom. They're just getting back on their feet here."

He exhales sharply and goes on. "Duty to kingdom was drilled into me since birth, so it was probably the only answer I could've heard and not released the kraken." He smiles a little, seeming proud he threw some slang into his formal speech. Good thing he managed to restrain himself. "Still, I wasn't ready to give up. I told them about your plans to build neighborhoods and give back to the community with parks and playgrounds as part of development. Anna offered to donate toward the parks and playgrounds through their charitable foundation. I accepted, of course, because it's a help, but I still wasn't happy. I was denied my place in the kingdom!"

He gives me a sideways glance. "I did release the kraken then, roaring my outrage. And that's when Anna said she thought she might be able to help. I didn't know what she was up to. Neither did Gabriel. Then she brought Mila to meet me and introduced me as her grandfather." His eyes well. "You see, the girl doesn't have a grandfather on either side. Just me. Anna only had her foster father, who also passed. Anna says being a grandfather to Mila will give me a new place in the kingdom and a second chance to experience childhood. They're trying to raise her as normally as possible, even though she'll one day be queen. Her training won't begin until she's sixteen. Times have changed on Villroy for the better."

I take that in for a moment. "Does that mean you're staying here?"

"No. I've made a good life for myself in Brooklyn, but I'll be a frequent visitor. I still plan on becoming a Realtor."

"So you gained a granddaughter."

He smiles widely and flutters the side of his velvet cape. "Yes. I'm enjoying child's play. I played with you and your brothers, too, but back then I was also working, and there was always someone who needed to be changed or fed or soothed. And I needed to be sure your mother wasn't doing too much. She was pregnant a lot of the time she was caring for you little ones."

"I was worried. I didn't hear from either of you."

He bumps my shoulder with his. "Never worry about me. I always land on my feet. I didn't want the distraction of my phone for such an important event, so I turned it off. Your mother was too busy trying to hold me back to spend time on her phone. She did say she texted you back, acknowledging that you were traveling here. After I connected with Mila, your mom went to the spa for the day with my sister-in-law, Princess Alexandra. They hit it off."

"So I guess I didn't need to fly here at all."

"No. That was your mother's worry about me that got you here, which was well-intentioned but misguided." He clasps my shoulder. "But I'm glad you're here. We'll all have dinner tonight. It's good for the cousins to connect. We're family."

I scratch the scruff on my jaw. Not saying I'm not happy for him, but I already had family. And now that he gave the crown and scepter back, I have no assets to move Rourke Management forward. I hate to start off in deep debt, but it's either that or stick with construction.

I need to talk to Ariana.

~

Ariana

"Mila is so adorable," I tell Dylan.

He's lying on the bed fully clothed with his arm over his eyes. "I know. She stole my dad's heart."

I touch up my lipstick in the vanity mirror. "So what's the plan? Now that you know your dad's okay, are we heading back tomorrow?"

"Sean's covering for me for a few days. I didn't know how long I'd have to be here. We can stay until the weekend if you want."

"Oh, I want. Get up. We've got dinner in the formal dining room. I'm thinking it's going to be fancy with the king and queen. How do I look?"

He pulls his arm off his eyes and stares at me in open admiration. "Gorgeous. I didn't know you brought a dress."

I'm wearing my little black dress. "Of course. You get invited to a royal palace, you have to bring something nice for the occasion."

He rolls out of bed and stalks toward me. "How long until we have to be downstairs?"

I back up a step, but he's faster, his arm snaking around my waist and pulling me flush against him. "Not long enough for that." My voice sounds breathy. It's hard to resist the heat of his hard body pressed against mine. "You need to change into something nice too."

His hand slides to the hem of my dress, sliding it up and caressing my leg at the same time. "This is as nice as it gets. Button-down shirt with trousers. No tie. Hate them."

I push his hand down from where it's now resting on my hip, his fingers toying with the side of my panties. "I can't show up to dinner looking like we just had sex."

He traces my collarbone and dips low to stroke the curve of one breast. My nipples harden into points. "Ariana, you know we need to practice baby-making."

I moan as his thumbs brush back and forth over my nipples. "We don't need any more practice."

His eyes gleam. "Lemme just try something out on ya."

My breath hitches. He's tricky using the same words as the first time we hooked up when he basically blew my mind and ruined me for all other men.

He grins devilishly and grabs me around the waist, lifting me right off the ground. I yelp in surprise even though his devilish look should've warned me. He carries me to the bed, sets me down on the side of it, and gives me a small shove backward. I land on my back on the soft mattress. Then he slides my dress up to my waist and yanks me by the hips to the edge of the mattress. My panties slide off a moment later.

"Open your legs for me, baby," he says, kneeling between them.

I smile. He maneuvers my body, he commands, he demands. But there's always this moment—a certain tone that tells me he's asking me to meet him halfway.

I spread my legs, and he rewards me with gruff praise before his hungry mouth consumes me.

"Do I look like you just fucked me seven ways to Sunday?" I ask him.

He grins.

I look in the mirror. I put myself back together, makeup,

hair, and all, but there's no getting around the flush to my cheeks and the red in my lips. Who knew multiple orgasms would be better than makeup? Still, it looks too obvious. I'm just too rosy, even my neck and chest.

I close my eyes and think cooling thoughts. His arms wrap around me from behind. "Don't worry. No one can see the bite marks."

"You're not helping me cool down. I think I'll go outside."

He nuzzles into my neck. "You've got beard burn too in a few places. Probably the worst on the side of your neck."

I dash to the mirror and apply more makeup to it. "That's the last time I'm letting you get me naked before a big event."

"Is it, though?" he whispers in my ear, coming up behind me and caressing my breasts until my nipples are hard and aching again. I should push him away, but my body softens, leaning against him.

"Dylan, please."

He releases me with a pat to my ass. I don't even squeak this time.

I look down at myself with my overly pointy nipples. "I need a shawl."

I grab a black crocheted shawl from my suitcase and drape it over myself to cover all the beard burn, bite marks, and pointy nipples. I jab a finger in his chest. "No more touching."

He gives me a slow smile, his hair sexily rumpled, his dark scruff giving him a dangerous edgy look. He's such a gorgeous man. "Can't help it when you look this sexy."

My lashes flutter down. "Thank you."

He takes my hand and guides me out of the room. "When we get back home, I'll get you a ring to make it official."

I stop in the hallway and tilt my head, studying him. "Are you proposing to me right now?"

"No. This is just so you know what's up. I'll get the ring when we get back home."

"So you're just telling me how it's gonna be."

"Yeah. Keeping you in the loop."

"Wow."

"Yeah." He gives my hand a squeeze, completely missing my sarcasm.

"Sometimes you're not very romantic."

His brows shoot up. "Whatta ya mean? Did I or did I not agree on our first date it would be cool with me to be your baby daddy given some conditions?"

"You did," I allow.

"Did I slow dance with you?"

"Yes."

"Did I share intimacies at your request?"

I giggle. "Yes, but then you got me naked."

"You begged me to help you out." His voice rises to a falsetto. "Please, Dylan, get me off. It's been so-o-o long. I ne-e-ed you!"

"Shh." I cover his mouth with my hand.

He shifts my hand away, yanks me against him, and kisses me breathless.

Long moments later, he frames my face with his big hands, his eyes intent on mine. "I love you. Marry me. Be mine and only mine until death do us part."

My heart thunders in my chest. I'm momentarily speechless. It's the most romantic thing I've ever heard, and it's from the guy who moments ago just casually informed me I'd be marrying him.

"Yes!" I cry. "Yes, I will. Happily so."

He smiles against my mouth before kissing me. "You'll get the ring when we get home. Like I told ya."

I laugh. His intention was there, the emotions were there, and he found the words I needed to hear. "Oh, Dylan. I'm starting to see you bring it all, even when I'm not sure you are. I'm starting to understand you."

"I'm not all that complicated." He takes my hand, and we head down the hallway. "What kind of ring do you want?"

"I don't want you to spend a lot. My ex spent a fortune..." I trail off. I still have that engagement ring. It's fifteen carats and worth a million dollars at least.

"Yeah, we all heard about your rich husband."

"His family was rich. They gifted us the house, so he

could spend more on my ring. It was a status thing." I halt. "Dylan, I still have that ring. I can sell it and invest it in property for Rourke Management. It'll get you started." I bounce on the balls of my feet. "I planned to use it for the sperm bank and to buy a place, but now you're my sperm, and you've got a place."

"I'm your sperm," he echoes, completely missing the fabulous point.

"You're my love, my baby daddy, my husband, my partner, my friend, my everything!" I throw my arms around his neck and kiss him.

He lifts his head. "You sure you want to use your money for me?"

"For us."

He hugs me. "Thank you, Ariana. You're everything I've ever wanted. You're mine." He smooths my hair back over my bare shoulder, his fingers trailing along my skin. "You know what I mean when I say you're mine?"

"Yes. We're loyal to each other. Faithful."

"Yeah, and you're my responsibility. I'll take care of you, protect you, love you. Anything you want I'll give because all I want is your happiness."

Tears leak out of my eyes, and he brushes them away with his thumbs. "You're truly a prince. And I'm the luckiest woman in the world."

He kisses me tenderly. "Ya feel like bailing on the formal dinner? I have it on good authority there's a gift for ya back in the room." His eyes sparkle devilishly, and I'm onto him.

I smile. "Is the gift six inches long?"

He smirks. "Let's call it a solid eight."

I shake my head, laughing. "Dinner."

Ariana

When we arrive in the dining room, the royal family is already seated with drinks. "Sorry we're late," I say and then curtsy. I heard that's what you're supposed to do when you see the king and queen. I know what they look like. I was one of those royal fans who watched their wedding on TV, but it's completely different to meet them in person.

At the end of a long gleaming table I meet the eyes of King Gabriel. He's clean shaven, his thick dark brown hair neatly trimmed, wearing a charcoal blazer over a white dress shirt, open at the collar. His sharp cheekbones, straight nose, and square jaw so closely resemble Dylan's face it's like they were stamped from the same mold. I hadn't made the family connection until seeing him in person.

"Not late," King Gabriel assures me. "We wanted to make sure Mila ate something before getting distracted by company. We've only had drinks."

"Drink!" Mila exclaims from her high chair adjacent to King Gabriel. She bangs her plastic sippy cup on the tray before taking a sip from it.

"Less banging, please," Gabriel says sternly.

She smiles around her sippy cup at her dad, and water

dribbles out the sides of her mouth. He takes a cloth napkin and dabs her dry.

"So nice to see you again, Dylan," Queen Anna says. "And nice to meet you too." She smiles at me from where she's sitting on Gabriel's other side. Her dark brown hair is long and curly, framing a heart-shaped face with sparkling brown eyes and creamy skin. I can see where her daughter got her coloring from.

"You too. I'm Ariana."

"My fiancée," Dylan says, placing a hand on the small of my back and guiding me straight to the head of the table to meet them.

I can't help my wide smile. "Yes. It just happened. He proposed."

Gabriel and Anna stand to congratulate us. Gabriel shakes Dylan's hand and claps him on the back. Anna even hugs me. The Queen of Villroy hugged me! And we just met!

"Have a seat and tell me how he did it," Anna says, gesturing for me to sit next to her. "Did he get down on one knee?"

"It was in the hallway on the way here," I say enthusiastically. "No bended knee, but that's okay."

"Oh," she says, glancing over at Dylan sitting on my other side.

"It was so romantic," I assure her. "He says he only cares for my happiness."

Dylan takes my hand and gives it a squeeze. I glance back at him with a smile before turning back to Anna.

"Ooh, let me see the ring!" she exclaims, gesturing for my hand.

"No ring yet," Dylan says. "I'll get one when we get back home."

"Sounds like it was very spontaneous," Gabriel says. "Congratulations again. Let's get some champagne to celebrate." He signals to a waiting servant, who bows his head and leaves the room.

"Here comes the tickle monster!" a voice booms.

We all turn to see Mr. Rourke with his hands wiggling

over his head, looking completely unscary and frankly ridiculous as he takes big monster steps into the room.

Mila lets out a bloodcurdling shriek of delight. "Pop-Pop!" She lifts her arms to be picked up, bouncing in her seat.

Mrs. Rourke follows him in at a sedate pace. "Hello, everyone!" She bends to kiss Dylan's cheek. She turns to me and kisses my cheek too. "Glad to see you both here."

"You too, Mrs. Rourke," I say.

"Please call me Tara."

"Okay, Tara," I say, trying it out.

She smiles. "My husband is Daniel, but he's a little more formal. Better wait for his go-ahead on that one."

Mila squeals as she's released from her high chair by her dad and lifted into Mr. Rourke's arms. She clasps his face with both hands on his cheeks and stares into his eyes.

"Boo," he says.

"Boo!" she yells right in his face.

"Mila! Inside voice!" Anna orders.

"Boo," Mila whisper-shouts. "Boo, boo, boo. Okay, Mama?"

"Good job," Anna says. "We don't want Pop-Pop to get hard of hearing from too much shouting."

Mila checks in Mr. Rourke's ear. He laughs.

A few minutes later, everyone's seated with Mila sitting on Mr. Rourke's lap.

The servant returns with a tray full of champagne glasses.

"I love champagne," Tara says. "What's the occasion?"

"Ariana and I are engaged," Dylan says. "I don't have—"

"Ahh!" Tara exclaims, throwing her arms out toward us from across the table. "When did this happen? I'm so excited for you!"

I walk around the table to hug her since her arms are still out. Mr. Rourke gives my arm a squeeze and congratulates us too.

"Does your mother know?" she asks me.

"It literally just happened right before we got to the dining room. He proposed in the hall. I'll let her know after dinner. At first, he just *told* me we were getting married." I shoot

Dylan a mock glare. "Then he made it romantic with a real proposal."

Dylan just smiles as he joins us.

Mr. Rourke grins. "I told Tara I was going to marry her on our first date."

"He did!" Tara exclaims. "I thought he was nuts! He was supposed to marry a princess he'd never met. It was all arranged."

"I knew you were meant for me the moment I clapped eyes on you," Mr. Rourke says tenderly. "She was mine."

"Mine!" Mila exclaims.

Tara beams. "I knew he was the man I'd always hoped for, but I didn't want to get between him and his destiny. That's when he told me *I* was his destiny." Her eyes tear up as she gazes at him for a long moment before turning back to us. "It all worked out. I'm so glad I got to spend some time with Princess Alexandra. She had to marry Daniel's brother instead, and she told me how happy they were together."

"My parents were very close," Gabriel says.

"A toast to true love," Anna exclaims, picking up her champagne glass.

Dylan and I head back to our seats to lift our glasses too. Once everyone lifts their glasses, Mr. Rourke says, "To true love and new family connections."

Everyone toasts and takes a drink. Mila holds up her sippy cup, and we all take turns tapping it before she sips her drink too.

Dinner is delightful, and I spend most of it chatting with Anna. She's American and has been wanting to show Mila around there as soon as she's old enough to appreciate it. I tell her all about the San Francisco area, which she's never been to, as well as fun things to do with kids in New York. The Bronx Zoo is a must. By the time a dessert course of chocolate blackout cake is served, I feel like Anna and I are old friends, and I actually find myself sharing about my future plans with Dylan and how I'm glad my old engagement ring can help launch our future together.

"It's like beautiful karma," she says. "What once was a sad reminder of an ending becomes a joyful new beginning."

"Exactly!"

"Anna," Gabriel says, inclining his head toward Mila, who's twirling a lock of hair around her finger and leaning against Mr. Rourke's shoulder.

Anna nods and turns to me. "Hair twirling means it's almost time for bed. I have to get Mila started on her bath and bedtime routine. It was so great talking to you. Please do keep in touch."

"I will. Oh! You should come to our wedding! Wouldn't it be so nice for the Villroy Rourkes to visit the American Rourkes in Brooklyn?"

"I'd love that!" She turns to Gabriel, who smiles and inclines his head. She turns back to me. "We'll be there."

I turn to Dylan, belatedly realizing I should've checked in with him since it was only recently that he reconnected with this side of his family.

"That works," he says. "Just don't expect a grand ballroom. It'll be low key."

"No, not like a palace wedding," I say with a laugh.

"You could marry here if you like," Anna says. "We have a chapel."

Like a real princess! I turn to Dylan to see what he thinks of the idea.

He leans close. "You'd like to be a princess bride, wouldn't ya?"

I nod vigorously. It's almost too much to hope for. Marrying my prince in the palace chapel. I saw it when I watched Gabriel and Anna marry there on TV a few years back. It's spectacular with a long red velvet runner, three gold-trimmed organs, marble statues, and hand-carved pews. My mother would be beside herself.

"Thank you," Dylan says. "We accept."

I squeal and throw my arms around him. Then I throw my arms around Anna. "I'm so excited!"

She laughs. "Me too! We'll make an official royal announcement that Prince Dylan will marry here in his family's chapel. The press should be good for everyone. We'll get plenty of attention on Villroy and our business ventures, and you may attract press for your company with the royal connection paving the way. I don't think there's any reason not to let the world know you're one of us now that everyone has reconciled, do you?"

"Agreed," I say. "Everyone should know the royal Rourkes from Brooklyn."

"Dad?" Dylan asks. "You okay with this?"

He smiles. "Absolutely."

Anna stands and crosses to her daughter, lifting her into her arms. Mila starts twirling Anna's hair. "And I love the idea you had of building parks and playgrounds with your development. Maybe one day Mila will play there."

"That would be wonderful!" I exclaim.

Dylan agrees gruffly.

Gabriel and Anna take their leave.

Mr. Rourke eyes Dylan. "It's not a handout to accept a charitable donation for a good cause. And don't underestimate the appeal of royalty, especially in the US. They love the fact that one of their own is queen." He puts an arm around his wife. "There was a time I wished it was your mother who was the beloved American queen, but it wasn't meant to be."

Tara pipes up. "Daniel, if I were queen, you would've been bound by duty to your kingdom. Instead you got to be involved with our kids. And we had a lot of fun."

He kisses her. "We did. Still do."

Dylan and I exchange an amused look. We know what kind of fun they like to have right in the living room.

"We're gonna call it a night," Tara says. "How long will you be here?"

"We'll be around until Sunday," I say.

"Maybe we'll fly back with you," she says. "If I can peel him away from his granddaughter. A new grandbaby would give him some incentive to stick around Brooklyn." She winks.

"That's the plan," Dylan says.

I silently thank him for not sharing how we first came up

with that plan. Me with baby fever asking for his sperm. I nearly cringe at the memory. He's so much more than a fine specimen.

The moment his parents leave, I tell Dylan, "Let's go check out the chapel."

"Sure. I know the way. I was there for Adrian's wedding." He takes my hand, and we head out.

"Are you okay with everything?" I ask. "The public royal connection, us getting married here, Villroy's donation to playgrounds?"

"Ya know, I think I am. Dad seems at peace with everything, and that gives me peace of mind too. He's the one who was hurt the most by the exile, and it seems he's been brought back into the fold even closer now."

"Amazing the wounds one toddler can heal."

"He musta been ready to heal."

"This is the right thing. For us, for your business, the perfect way forward."

"And all because of you."

I press a hand to my chest. "Me? It wasn't me who brought everyone together."

"Without you there is no wedding at the palace chapel. Without you there is no money from a ridiculously expensive engagement ring. Without you there is no love to remind everyone why we value each other and family."

I throw myself into his arms and pepper kisses all over his face. "I love you, I love you, I love you. My sweet romantic prince of a man."

He cups my bottom. "You forgot sexy."

I give him a knowing look. "That's how this all began."

He grabs me, lifting me off the ground and spinning me around. I yelp, and then I laugh, giddy with pure joy.

When we get to the chapel, it's locked. Dylan wastes no time finding an unlocked window around back and hoisting himself through it. He lets me in through the front door.

I take a moment to admire it, slowly walking down the red runner in the center aisle. He joins me in the center under the glow of a candelabra, his arm banding around my waist, his other hand holding mine. We dance, a slow sway of warmth and love, one of many more to come. He's my dance partner, my life partner, my lover, my prince.

His voice is a dark rumble in my ear. "Would lightning strike me down if I took you here?"

"Yes!" My prince has a one-track mind.

He kisses me. "Was that a yes to taking you here?" His eyes sparkle in the dim light, a smile tugging at his lips.

I shake my head at him and then squeak as he scoops me up and carries me back down the aisle. "What about our dance?"

"You can only expect me to hold you close for so long before you wake the beast. Listen, I got plans for you once I get you naked. Don't worry. It's all perfectly normal."

"I can't believe you remember so much of what you said to me the first time we hooked up. That's exactly what you said before. Don't worry. It's all normal."

"Course I remember. It played like a porno film in my mind for months."

"I'm not sure how I feel about starring in your porno."

"Baby, you belong there. Place of honor." And then he proceeds to tell me in explicit filthy detail what he plans to do to me.

I bury my face in his neck, nearly squirming with the fire of raw lust coursing through me.

"Aww, you're feeling shy," he says. "I'll get you hot enough to drop your inhibitions. I always do."

I bite his neck, and he groans.

The moment we leave the chapel, he takes my hand, and we make a mad dash back to the palace.

We collide in our room and grab for each other urgently.

"I love you," I say, ripping his shirt off.

"I worship you," he says, ripping my dress off.

"You cherish me," I tell him as he tosses me over his shoulder.

"You beg me." He caresses my bottom as he carries me to the bed. "Baby, I love when you do that."

And moments later I do. And I love it too.

EPILOGUE

Two months later…

Dylan

I'm really digging the luxury of flying on the private jet. It's just me, Ariana, my best man, her matron of honor, and our parents. After our wedding on Villroy, Ariana and I are taking the jet to Italy for our honeymoon. Everyone else will have to fly home the regular way. Some nice perks to being royal. Sean's my best man since we're closest in age. I told my brothers to choose each other on down the line in age order as best man so no one gets bent out of shape. When Sean gets married, he'll choose Jack and so on. Even if they don't get married in age order, they can still be best man in age order. Beast (Garrett) is too young at twenty-three to be ready to settle down. Maybe I'll be his best man one day, bringing it full circle.

We landed a few minutes ago, and we'll be heading to the yacht next to take us to the island. Ariana's mother has been taking pictures nonstop, even of the warm chocolate chip cookie they served us on the jet. She's been sharing on social media and tagging our new Rourke Management account that Ariana set up. Between the two of them and the press that's been covering our "true-life fairy tale," I'm sure we won't have any problem getting word of mouth going for Rourke Management.

Once we get out on the tarmac, waiting for our luggage, I hear Sean on his phone. "I told ya I'm not finished with renovating. It's not *livable*. You can't—" He scowls. "I know I've been living there. I'm the contractor. No one can buy it yet." Pause. "I understand, but…no. Winnie, you're not listening."

He goes on like this a few more rounds, getting louder and louder before he jolts and stares at the phone. "She hung up on me."

"Is she evicting you?" I ask. He's been renovating his ex's place in exchange for free rent for months now. He can only work on it on the weekends since he's busy during the week at his paying job.

He gestures at his phone. "She wants me to hurry up and finish so she can sell. So, yeah, basically I'm getting evicted. I can't hurry up."

"You can have it fast, or you can have it right," I say just like our uncle Pat used to say to clients.

"Exactly!" He shoves a hand through his hair. "Just because her fiancé is pressuring her. All he cares about is money."

"You have to let her go," I say. "Sticking around your old place with her is still hanging on." I've tried talking to him about this before. Winnie lives in the city with her Wall Street guy, but she still owns her house in Brooklyn, where Sean's staying. She inherited it from her grandmother.

Sean frowns. "I'm not hanging on. I want to finish the job, and I'm looking for a new place. Nothing good's come up on the market."

"Because you want to live in a neighborhood you can't afford."

His eyes narrow. "Don't you have a bride to hover over?"

I knock his shoulder and spot Ariana talking to her mom. Mrs. Bianchi insists I call her Ma like Ariana, but I can't bring myself to do it. Ariana gives me a small smile, and her mother turns, giving me a hard look.

I blow out a breath. Ariana confessed. I told her to wait until after the wedding.

I cross to her, wrap an arm around her shoulders, and pull her close. I'll take the heat for this one. It's not Ariana's fault she loses her mind when I touch her. That's just my powerful sex appeal. Although this time she basically ripped my clothes off and impaled herself on me. That's what happens when you take a former good girl to see your first property for development—an old school we're going to turn into cool office space—and send her to the principal's office. She so wanted to be bad.

"It's true," I say. "She's pregnant. I know it's before the wed—"

"Pregnant!" Mrs. Bianchi exclaims, throwing her hands in the air. "Ah! Tara! Get over here for this wonderful news!"

I glance down at Ariana, who shakes her head. "Dylan, we said we weren't gonna tell people yet."

"What were ya telling her before? She gave me a dark look, so I thought she was mad about it. I was taking the heat for ya!"

She leans against my side. "I told her you weren't cool with the pink boutonnière she wanted you to wear to match my bouquet."

"Oops."

"Big oops."

"Can you convince her not to announce it publicly until after the wedding?"

She pats my chest. "All you. You're the one who blabbed."

I grin down at her. "You're the one who was a very bad girl."

She grabs my shirt by the collar and pulls me down for a kiss. "Worth it."

Our parents descend on us a moment later in a flurry of congratulations, kisses, and hugs. Ah, family. I can't imagine a better one to join with. Turns out Bianchis and Rourkes do mix.

≈

Ariana

I am a legit princess walking down the aisle in my flowing white gown to my prince. Uh-uh, don't tell me he's only half a prince because of his commoner blood. No way. My man is all prince and he's mine, all mine.

I should be more nervous. It's a big deal that the first Rourke from his father's side is marrying in the family chapel. There's TV cameras in here and a slew of reporters outside. We agreed it was good for both of the families and their businesses to make our union public. All I care about is marrying the man who was always meant for me.

My father escorts me to my prince and congratulates us both, kissing my cheek before taking his seat with my mother. I glance back and see them holding hands. My mother and Dylan's mother exchange a weepy smile. Fences are mended. Good thing too because I did *not* want to negotiate grandchildren privileges between two strong-willed women.

Dylan holds my jaw, his blue eyes smoldering into mine. "You look beautiful."

Emotion clogs my throat. "You too," I choke out and tears escape. "Handsome, I mean."

He smiles warmly. I want to hug him, but he turns to the minister and it's time.

Next thing I know, I'm Princess Ariana Rourke. Oh, yeah, they gave me the title. I'm an American princess, and my man makes me feel like one every day.

He kisses me, bending me back over his arm and then pulling me back up. He's playing to our audience. If it was just us, he would've gone for a deep kiss, and his hands would be all over me.

The moment we step outside, lights blind me as photo flashes go off. "How's it feel to be royalty?" a reporter asks.

"It feels like I just joined a wonderful family," I say.

"More to come," Dylan says.

"You mean your brothers?" another reporter asks.

Dylan and I exchange a secret look because we both mean more to come in our little family.

"Among other things," he says and guides me to the

waiting horse and carriage for the short ride to the palace ballroom.

The press is abuzz about his brothers. Who knows, maybe one of them will one day marry here too.

It's a dream come true for me. For both of us.

Don't miss the next book in the series *Rogue Gentleman*, where Sean gets an unexpected roommate!

Josie

I'm an actress between gigs crashing on the couch at my cousin's old place. I won't be here forever. I just filmed a pilot and, if the show gets picked up, I'm off to LA for my dream job. Only I never expected my new roommate would be the grouchiest man on earth. It almost cancels out his sexy rugged good looks. Almost.

Sean

The last thing I need is a woman moving into the house I'm renovating on the side. First of all, I live here. Second, I'm running on fumes trying to juggle my day job too. I don't have time for her irritating cheer or her distractingly cute little body. I've got work to do.

And then Josie decides to "help" me renovate, which has the aggravating effect of making more work for me. I'm losing my damn mind. Yet, somehow, I can't stop looking at her.

Sign up for my newsletter to be emailed when *Rogue Gentleman* releases at kyliegilmore.com/newsletter

ALSO BY KYLIE GILMORE

Happy Endings Book Club Series
Hidden Hollywood (Book 1)
Inviting Trouble (Book 2)
So Revealing (Book 3)
Formal Arrangement (Book 4)
Bad Boy Done Wrong (Book 5)
Mess With Me (Book 6)
Resisting Fate (Book 7)
Chance of Romance (Book 8)
Wicked Flirt (Book 9)
An Inconvenient Plan (Book 10)
A Happy Endings Wedding (Book 11)

The Clover Park Series
The Opposite of Wild (Book 1)
Daisy Does It All (Book 2)
Bad Taste in Men (Book 3)
Kissing Santa (Book 4)
Restless Harmony (Book 5)
Not My Romeo (Book 6)
Rev Me Up (Book 7)
An Ambitious Engagement (Book 8)
Clutch Player (Book 9)
A Tempting Friendship (Book 10)
Clover Park Bride: A Clover Park Short
A Valentine's Day Gift (Book 11)
Maggie Meets Her Match (Book 12)

The Clover Park STUDS Series

Almost Over It (Book 1)

Almost Married (Book 2)

Almost Fate (Book 3)

Almost in Love (Book 4)

Almost Romance (Book 5)

Almost Hitched (Book 6)

The Rourkes Series

Royal Catch (Book 1)

Royal Hottie (Book 2)

Royal Darling (Book 3)

Royal Charmer (Book 4)

Royal Player (Book 5)

Royal Shark (Book 6)

Rogue Prince (Book 7)

Rogue Gentleman (Book 8)

ABOUT THE AUTHOR

Kylie Gilmore is the *USA Today* bestselling author of the Rourkes series, the Happy Endings Book Club series, the Clover Park series, and the Clover Park STUDS series. She writes humorous romance that makes you laugh, cry, and reach for a cold glass of water.

Kylie lives in New York with her family, two cats, and a nutso dog. When she's not writing, wrangling kids, or dutifully taking notes at writing conferences, you can find her flexing her muscles all the way to the high cabinet for her secret chocolate stash.

Thanks for reading *Rogue Prince.* I hope you enjoyed it. Would you like to know about new releases? You can sign up for my new release email list at kyliegilmore.com/newsletter. I promise not to clog your inbox! Only new release info, sales, and some fun giveaways.

I love to hear from readers! You can find me at:
    kyliegilmore.com
    Instagram.com/kyliegilmore
    Facebook.com/KylieGilmoreToo
    Twitter @KylieGilmoreToo

If you liked Dylan and Ariana's story, please leave a review on your favorite retailer's website or Goodreads. Thank you.

www.ingramcontent.com/pod-product-compliance
Lightning Source LLC
Chambersburg PA
CBHW070956180726
48291CB00004B/1323